QUESTIONS AND ANSWERS ON
PREGNANCY

QUESTIONS AND ANSWERS ON
PREGNANCY

Nutan Pandit

ASSOCIATE
THE NATIONAL CHILDBIRTH TRUST
LONDON

RUPA

Published by
Rupa Publications India Pvt. Ltd 2007
7/16, Ansari Road, Daryaganj
New Delhi 110002

Sales centres:
Allahabad Bengaluru Chennai
Hyderabad Jaipur Kathmandu
Kolkata Mumbai

ISBN: 978-81-291-1110-4

Sixth impression 2019

10 9 8 7 6

Nutan Pandit asserts the moral right to be identified

All material and sources by author.

For
my sister Indu and her husband Satti Punj.
Thanks for being there for me.

Contents

Acknowledgements

I am grateful to all those who have freely shared their knowledge to make this book possible. May they be blessed!

I have sourced information for over twenty-eight years from books, doctors, conferences, workshops, internet, friends, students, traditional birth attendants and so on. It would be impossible to mention everyone, but they stand acknowledged and appreciated.

Nutan Lakhanpal Pandit

Preface

In my twenty-nine years of conducting natural childbirth classes, I have often been asked questions by expectant couples, couples who are planning to have a baby, curious people, breastfeeding mothers, grandparents, etc. In this book I have strived to answer most of these questions in the hope that it can clear doubts and provide useful information.

The author conducts natural childbirth classes at:

D-178, Defence Colony, New Delhi 110 024
Tel: 24690552, 24601689
E-mail: nutanpandit@yahoo.com
Website: www.ncbchildbirth.com

1
Conception

Q1.   How does one 'plan' a baby?

Ans.   When you decide to have a baby, you need to 'plan' to have one. Stop using all kinds of contraceptives, be it the pill, condoms or Copper T. If you are diabetic, your condition will need to be assessed before your pregnancy to avoid complications later on. If you are anaemic, try and improve your diet to increase your haemoglobin level before getting pregnant. The husband and wife should both avoid cigarettes and alcohol.

Q2.   How many times a week is intercourse recommended in order to have a baby?

Ans.   Fourteen days before your next menstrual period is due, you are liable to get pregnant. Two weeks before your next period is due, you can have unprotected intercourse daily for one week. You can also go off on a private holiday with your husband and have frequent intercourse, since sexual stimulation can make the ovary expel an ovum.

Strictly by the book, intercourse should happen within a day or two after ovulation. To check when you ovulate, you can take your temperature before getting out of bed in the morning. If your temperature is slightly higher, you have ovulated. The temperature rises very slightly.

Q3.   If I am using contraceptives, i.e. pills, when do I stop them? After how long can I conceive?

Ans.   You can conceive immediately the month after you stop having contraceptive pills. It is best if your husband starts using a condom and spermicidal pessary for two to three months, or more after you stop the pill so that all hormones are out of your system by the time you conceive.

Q4.   Is it advisable to use the pill soon after getting married?

Ans.   The pill is advisable soon after marriage because its failure rate is nil. It should be started one menstrual cycle before marriage so that a woman gets used to having it. She can take a multivitamin with it containing vitamin B6, folic acid, calcium, manganese, zinc and ascorbic acid.

Six months after taking the pill, when a woman is a little more familiar with her body, she can switch to condoms and spermicidal pessaries for two months so that her body gets a break from having hormones regularly. Then she can go back to the pill. She should have a break every six months.

Q5. **Does having the pill lead to infertility and weight gain?**

Ans. Having the pill does not lead to infertility or the chances of not conceiving a baby as is commonly believed. However, it is possible that a woman who is already infertile may be taking the pill and she becomes aware that she is infertile only after she stops taking it.

Just as some people are sensitive to certain drugs, some women may be sensitive to taking the pill. One of the possible side-effects can be weight gain. Other possible side-effects can be nausea, fluid retention, enlarged and painful breasts, change in sexual desire and/or fungus infection of the vagina. Should these symptoms arise, you could discuss with your doctor or a family planning centre about switching to another contraceptive.

Q6. **Is using the Copper T safe before your first pregnancy?**

Ans. Copper T is not recommended before the first pregnancy.

Q7. **How long does it take to conceive?**

Ans. One may conceive immediately on having unprotected intercourse or may take several months to conceive.

Q8.   After how many years of marriage should one panic if the woman fails to conceive?

Ans.   If a woman fails to conceive for two years even after having unprotected intercourse, it is advisable to seek the help of a specialist who deals with infertility. Further, if you are keen to conceive and for one year have had unprotected intercourse twice a week and yet not conceived, you may consult your doctor.

Q9.   What are the causes for not conceiving?

Ans.   If either a man or a woman is severely malnourished, conception may not happen. Also, if either of them is suffering from an infection, like tuberculosis of the reproductive tract, taking certain drugs for treatment, conception may be hampered. Given below are some common reasons that cause infertility. However, there may be several other reasons that investigations may reveal.

REASONS WHY A MAN WILL NOT CAUSE PREGNANCY

A man may not cause pregnancy if he has a low sperm count. That is, when a man ejaculates, there are several million sperm in the semen or the fluid that is ejaculated. Out of these, only one manages to pierce or impregnate the ovum or 'seed' in the mother's body. However, due to pollution and modern day lifestyles, the sperm count can reduce and conception may not happen. For example, when men wear synthetic underwear and sit for long hours in the heat, like travelling for hours daily by bus or train in the hot weather, they can develop varicose veins in the testes due to excessive heat, and this can destroy the sperm. On the other hand, some men may have damaged sperm.

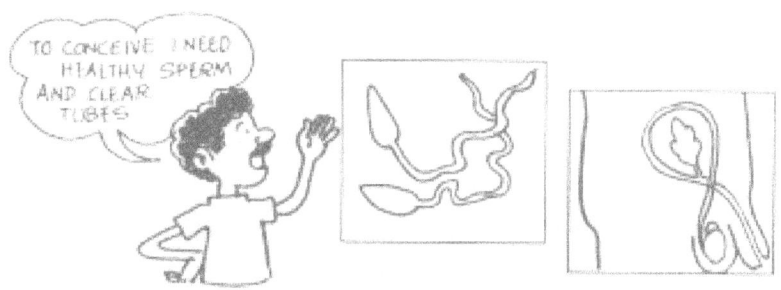

Sometimes, a man may be impotent, that is, he may not perform sexually, and therefore not be able to cause pregnancy.

A man may also not be able to cause pregnancy if there is a blockage of the tubes between the testes and the penis.

REASONS WHY A WOMAN WILL NOT CONCEIVE

A woman's fallopian tubes, through which the sperm travels to meet the ovum, may be blocked. In fact, any interference with the fallopian tubes such as an ectopic pregnancy, adhesions after abdominal surgery or pelvic inflammatory diseases can block the tubes and prevent fertilisation of the ovum by the sperm.

Further, multiple fibroids or endometriosis may do the same.

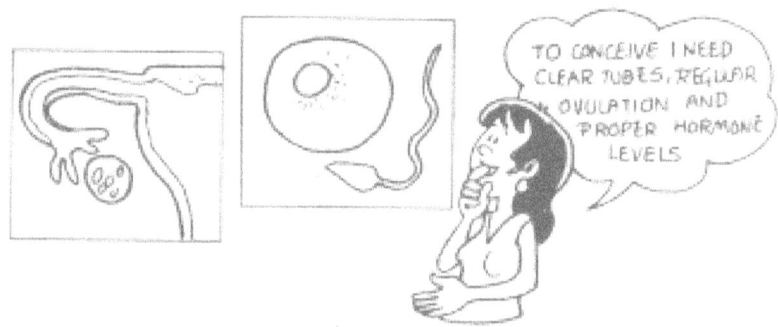

A fibroid is a benign tumour of fibrous and muscular tissue, one or more of which may develop in the muscular wall of the womb.

Fibroids often cause pain and excessive menstrual bleeding, and they may become extremely large. They are not life-threatening but make pregnancy unlikely. Sometimes fibroids may not be very big and may not give rise to any symptoms either.

A woman may also not conceive if her hormone level is disturbed or if her body does not release an ovum, that is, if she does not ovulate.

Q10. How can one plan a healthy baby?

Ans. When you plan to have a baby, it is important that both the man and the woman are in good health and well-nourished. A nutritious diet, less stress, less alcohol and cigarettes, less lead exhaust from vehicles, less caffeine from tea, coffee and cola drinks, no indiscriminate use of drugs, are all factors that will contribute to a strong and healthy baby. Check these factors three to six months before conception, specially approximately fifteen days before the next cycle is due, because pregnancy starts at that time. A man's diet, smoking and drinking habits, etc. can harm his sperm. A woman needs to check these factors throughout pregnancy.

Q11. **If a woman is used to living in the plains and for some reason (mostly in the case of army officers' wives) she has to live on high altitude, is it safe for her to conceive there?**

Ans. At high altitudes, the oxygen in the air is less. As far as a man is concerned, spending a long time on high altitudes or being exposed to excessive high temperature or heat can affect the production of sperm.

Maybe if a woman gets pregnant, she can shift back to the plains. It is an interesting fact that the placentas of the local population on high altitudes are larger. (A placenta is an organ that nourishes the baby and is delivered after the baby is born.)

Q12. **How do twins happen?**

Ans. Twins can happen when one ovum splits into two. Such twins are identical and of the same sex. They share a placenta, but have their own cords and sacs.

Twins can also happen when two ova are fertilised by two different sperm. These have their separate placentas and can be a boy and a girl. They are like two separate children of the same parents.

Q13. What is the ideal age to have a baby?

Ans.   Fertility in a man and a woman diminishes after the age of twenty-five. In a woman, there is a definite decline in fertility after thirty years of age. After forty-five, only half her menstrual periods are accompanied by ovulation or release of an ovum.

Sometimes two partners may not conceive because, say, the man may have a low sperm count and since the woman is fertile only for two to three days a month, intercourse may be badly timed or the woman's age may be against her. However, if either has a new partner whose high fertility can compensate for the low fertility of the earlier partner, conception may be possible..

Further, if intercourse is resorted to after a gap of some days, the sperm count builds up and increases fertility. Fertility in a man declines with age also, but not as sharply as in a woman.

2
Pregnancy

Q14. How do I know I am pregnant?

Ans. The simplest way of knowing that you are pregnant is a missed period.

A blood or urine test can also help to detect a pregnancy. The blood or urine is tested for the presence of HCG hormone which gets released in the body during pregnancy. For the urine test to be reliable, it needs to be carried out two weeks after a missed period. For an immediate result, a blood test is more reliable.

Some women may feel nauseous when they get pregnant, may need to urinate more frequently or feel tenderness in the breasts.

A doctor can detect a pregnancy by clinically examining a woman. A woman who is pregnant will have an enlarged uterus, softening of genital organs and during an internal vaginal examination, the cervix or mouth of the uterus will look purplish velvety.

Q15. When do I start seeing a doctor?

Ans. Some women who are very aware see their doctors from the beginning of their pregnancies, while some who undergo fertility tests may start seeing their doctors before pregnancy.

On the other hand, there are also women who go to see a doctor only after they are three months pregnant. A doctor practising privately can be contacted or else, one can visit an out-patient department (OPD) in a hospital or medical centre.

Q16. Is sex safe during pregnancy?

Ans.   During a normal, stable pregnancy, there is no harm in having sex. However, if it is a 'precious pregnancy', one that may be after treatment for infertility or after many years of marriage, or if there has been bleeding or premature contractions, the doctor may ask a couple to avoid intercourse.

If the doctor asks you to avoid sex in pregnancy, you and your partner can instead lovingly stroke or massage each other. Apart from that, you can do other things together, like go for outings, have long chats with each other, do up the house together, go through old photographs together, etc.

Q17. Can one get pregnant without full penetration?

Ans.   Yes, one can get pregnant without full penetration of the male penis into the female vagina. Even if the penis leaks and the fluid is deposited on the outer lips of the vagina, the fluid can contain enough sperm that can gain entry into the vagina and cause a pregnancy.

Q18. If I get pregnant without full penetration, will my baby be abnormal?

Ans. No, the baby will not be abnormal.

Q19. Is it true that one can choose the sex of the baby?

Ans. French doctors Dr Papa and Dr Labro have written a book, *Boy or Girl? Choosing Your Child Through Your Diet* (Ritana Books, New Delhi). Doctors in Canada and France, who have been advocating the diet theory, feel that there is an eighty percent chance of success. Both partners need to adhere to a particular kind of diet a few months before conception.

For a girl, they advise a diet rich in starch, milk and milk products and low in salt. They also recommend taking a tablet of calcium everyday.

For a boy, they advise a diet high in salt, meat and fruits. A daily potassium tablet is also recommended.

The timing of intercourse can also influence the sex of the child. According to *The Complete Handbook of Pregnancy* (Sphere Books, 1984), 'Some researchers say that the closer to ovulation you have intercourse, the more likely you are to have a girl: about a sixty—rather than a fifty percent chance.

'An American gynaecologist and a British woman researcher each disagree with this. The latter, who claims an eighty percent success rate, says that the closer to ovulation intercourse occurs, the greater the chance of having a boy.'

Q20. How do I know if I have ovulated?

Ans. There are various methods by which ovulation can be detected in a woman. The cheapest, easiest and the most natural way is the temperature method. Before ovulation, a woman's body temperature dips slightly and when ovulation occurs, it rises slightly. A dip in the temperature signifies that the ovum is ready for release. A rise signifies the release of the ovum. The temperature has to be taken at the same time everyday. It has to be taken when you wake up in the morning, before getting out of bed and before taking any food or drink. The thermometer must be kept in place for a least three minutes.

It dips to one degree below the normal body temperature, and rises slightly above the normal body temperature. The temperature should therefore be taken by a very sensitive thermometer. The temperature will remain high until the next period begins.

One can start taking the temperature several months before planning a baby, and keeping a record of it, so that one can eventually pinpoint when ovulation occurs between the menstrual periods. This will also eliminate error that can happen if a woman suddenly comes up with an infection or fever.

Doctors can help pinpoint ovulation by clinically checking the cervical mucus or through ultrasound.

Q21.   How important are iron and calcium supplement tablets?

Ans.   Iron and calcium tablets are very important if you do not eat nutritious food. However, there is nothing like getting your nourishment from food that is best absorbed by the body. Natural sources of iron, calcium, protein are:

Protein	Calcium	Iron
Pulses (*Dals*)	Milk	*Kishmish* (raisins)
Soya bean	Curd	
Lentils (*rajma,*	Buttermilk	*Pudina* (mint)
channa, etc.)	*Paneer*	*Dhania* (coriander)
Sprouts	Raddish leaves	
Eggs (specially	Cauliflower	Raddish leaves
egg white)	leaves	*Poha/chidwa*
Fish	Oranges	Lotus stem
Meat/chicken	Sweet lemons	Dried fish
Missie roti	Lemons	Dried figs (*angir*)
(*roti, paratha*		Dried apricots
made with *besan*		
or *channa atta*)		

Q22. Is it good to eat fish when pregnant?

Ans.   Fish is excellent to eat when pregnant because it is rich in omega 3 fatty acids. A regular intake of omega 3 fatty acids enhances the intelligence of the child and reduces depression in the mother. Apart from fish, omega 3 fatty acids are also present in walnuts, soya bean oil and flaxseed oil. It is best to ingest omega 3 fatty acids through food and not through tablets. Women can eat a few walnuts daily.

A lot of pregnant American women avoid fish to avoid exposing the baby in the womb to trace amounts of brain damaging mercury poisoning that may be present in the fish. However, according to Dr Joseph Hibbeln from America's National Institutes of Health, omega 3 fatty acids show, 'that the benefits of eating such fish far outweigh the risks from mercury in them... the amount of omega 3 in a pregnant woman's diet helps to determine her child's intelligence, fine-motor skills (such as the ability to manipulate small objects, and hand-eye coordination) and also the propensity to anti-social behaviour'.

The Avon study was begun fifteen years ago (as on February 2006) by Jean Golding and contains data of fourteen thousand expectant mothers and their offspring. It showed that 'at 3½ years of age, those children with the best measures of fine-motor performance were the ones whose mothers had had the highest intake of omega 3s...a low intake of omega 3s during pregnancy led to higher levels of pathological social interactions such as an inability to make friends as a child grew up'.

Q23. Are tetanus injections important?

Ans. Tetanus injections given to a pregnant mother protect both the mother and the baby from tetanus infections for several months after the birth of the baby.

Q24. How much weight should one put on in pregnancy?

Ans. Earlier, 9 kilograms used to be considered the permitted weight gain in pregnancy. However, now it is considered to be 12 to 13 kilograms.

If you were underweight when you conceived or if you are going to have twins, you are likely to cross the permitted weight gain. Fried food and sweets can lead to unnecessary weight gain. Since these two food groups make you nauseous, ask others not to not force you to eat them.

The following is an estimate of expected weight increase in pregnancy:

Foetus and placenta	5.0 kg
Water	1 to 1.5 kg
Uterus	0.5 to 1.0 kg
Breasts	1 to 1.5 kg
Fat storage in tissues	4 to 4.5 kg
Total expected weight gain	**13.5 kg approx.**

Q25.   How can putting on extra weight be controlled?

Ans.   To avoid gaining excess weight, do not allow yourself to get hunger pangs. When you get hunger pangs, you are likely to eat unhealthy food. Eat regularly. If there is still time for a meal and you are hungry, eat a fruit or a bowl of curd. Do not eat when nervous. Take a walk or chew a chewing gum instead. Eat slowly and savour every morsel you eat by chewing your food well and experiencing its taste to the fullest.

If you are a compulsive eater, keep the right kind of snacks around, like *moong* sprouts, boiled potatoes, carrots, cucumber, seasonal fruits and *channas*. At meal time, serve yourself once, generously, then avoid refills.

Avoid fried food, creamy puddings, and sweets. Drink water instead of sweet cold drinks.

Q26.   Is it true that you should be happy and read good books, see pictures of happy babies in pregnancy?

Ans.   Yes, it is true that in pregnancy a mother should be happy and see good and happy things. Mythology is abundant with instances that tell us that what the mother sees and hears, when pregnant, affects the baby too.

All eastern cultures like the Indian, Japanese and Chinese stress that the mood and activities of a pregnant woman should be positive and happy.

Hippocrates, the father of medicine, also believed that a pregnant woman influences the baby she carries.

A pregnant woman releases different hormones with different emotional states. For instance, the chemistry in a woman's body who is happy will be different from the chemistry of one who is depressed. The baby who is living within the mother is affected by these emotions. The baby's chemistry also changes accordingly. It is, therefore, important that a pregnant woman be pampered and kept happy. If a pregnant woman happens to be living alone and away from people who would have pampered her, she needs to be pampered by her partner. If her partner travels extensively, she has one best friend she can rely upon always—that is, herself! Create an atmosphere of happiness for yourself— listen to your favourite music, eat your favourite food, visit your favourite people, read your favourite books (no negative books please!), do your favourite things. You owe it to yourself and your baby to be as happy as you can, since your baby would be greatly impacted.

A letter from a mother greatly illustrates this point:

> My due date was 11th November, and as you know, Ronnie arrived on the 12th. I must tell you a little incident that happened on the 11th when we went in for our last checkup. I was hooked up to the C.T.G. monitor, getting Ronnie's heart rate checked, when the nurse, who was chatting with my husband and me earlier, brought in a little baby girl who was just

born but was abandoned at the hospital by the mother. So while the police were investigating, the nurses on duty were taking care of the baby. My husband and I were horrified by the story, and he just reached out and carried the child when Ronnie's heart rate that was being successfully picked up by the machine, suddenly dropped! This triggered off the alarm and the nurses and the doctors came immediately with the oxygen cylinder, and we were advised to go in for a Caesarean because Ronnie appeared to be in trouble.

In the commotion, my husband had hurriedly returned the abandoned baby to the nurse and at the precise moment he did that, Ronnie's heart rate returned to normal. He immediately made a solemn promise to his possessive daughter that he would never be attentive to another baby besides her.

She certainly gave us a scare that night but she arrived the next day normally.

Q27. **1 am seven weeks pregnant, my tests show that progesterone levels are low. My doctor prescribed progesterone hormone to stabilise the pregnancy. My mother said not to take it but to wait for a month and then test the progesterone level again.**

Ans. Progesterone is produced in the first few weeks of pregnancy by the corpus luteum, or the follice that holds the egg or the ovum. If the egg is not fertilised within a few days, the follicle dries up and the progesterone levels fall dramatically. This causes the uterine lining to disintegrate and a menstrual period occurs.

'Progresterone is produced by the corpus luteum in the first few weeks of pregnancy. Thereafter, it is derived from the placenta, its output reaches a maximum of atleast 250 mg per day.' (*Obstetrics Illustrated*, Churchill Livingstone, 1980).

According to *Mayes' Midwifery* (1997), progesterone injections are sometimes given weekly during the first fourteen to sixteen weeks of pregnancy. 'However, there is no real evidence that this treatment is effective.'

Therefore, it is not very essential to take progesterone injections. You can reach your doctor if you experience spotting or bleeding. If a pregnancy happens, waiting it out could correct the hormone level naturally.

Q28. I have developed dark patches on my face and freckles with my pregnancy. Is this a permanent change?

Ans. It is common in pregnancy to develop dark patches on the face. There is also a general darkening in certain areas like the areola, the dark area behind the nipple, or the darkening of a line, starting from below the naval and ending at the pubic hair. Freckles, moles and scars may also darken. This happens because pregnancy hormones may enlarge dark pigments on the skin. Generally, these changes disappear after pregnancy but may remain in some instances.

Q29. My doctor asks me to have an aspirin daily during pregnancy. Should I?

Ans. There is no need to have an aspirin when you are pregnant. It used to be advised for a short while but its prescription has been discontinued. It serves no purpose. In pregnancy, the fluid volume or water in the blood naturally increases, rendering the blood thinner. Indiscriminate use of aspirin could lead to bleeding difficulties.

Q30. Why have I grown off non-vegetarian food ever since I have conceived?

Ans. A lot of women naturally go off non-vegetarian food when pregnant. It is probably their body telling them what it needs. Some women might suddenly want to eat non-vegetarian food. It is best to listen to your body and eat accordingly. The number of women going off non-vegetarian food is greater somehow. Good nutrition can also be had from vegetarian sources.

Q31. I have been told not to eat papaya and pineapple in pregnancy. Why?

Ans. A slice of papaya or a few pieces of pineapple can do no harm. Earlier, when medical science was not so advanced, large quantities of papayas were used to cause an abortion when a pregnancy was unwanted. Papaya does contain a little bit of ergometrine, a hormone used to induce labour. But to cause an abortion, one would probably need volumes of it.

Many women have had safe pregnancies with a daily slice of papaya for breakfast to keep constipation at bay.

Q32. I am RH negative and my doctor says that I will have to take some drugs after childbirth. Is it safe?

Ans. If your blood group is RH negative and your husband's blood group is RH positive, there are chances that your baby may also be RH positive.

When your baby is born, or in late pregnancy, the baby's blood may leak into your blood circulation. Your body will respond to the baby's blood as an enemy and will produce antibodies against it. If these antibodies leak back into the baby's circulation, they can destroy a large number of the baby's blood cells and cause severe anaemia and jaundice in the newborn. In order to avoid this from happening, an injection of anti D immunoglobulin can be given to a rhesus negative mother immediately after the birth of a rhesus positive baby. Given forty-eight hours after birth, it stops the mother's biological defence mechanism from acting against the baby's blood. A fresh injection is given after every delivery, miscarriage or abortion. It is possible for blood from an aborted foetus to enter the mother's bloodstream.

Nowadays, sometimes this injection is given during pregnancy. This applies only if the mother is RH negative and the father, RH positive, not vice versa.

Q33. I am three months pregnant and my colleague at work has measles. Should I avoid work?

Ans. Yes, avoid exposure to measles in pregnancy. In fact, if a woman gets measles in the first three months of her pregnancy, doctors advise a medical termination of pregnancy or abortion since its effect on the foetus can be grave. After the first three months, the effects are less grave but avoidable nonetheless. Tell your boss that it is doctor's orders that you stay away. Also stay away from friends or relatives if they have measles in the house.

Q34. **Is it true that an unborn child is affected during an eclipse?**

Ans. There is a strong belief that an unborn child is affected during an eclipse, and hence a woman is asked to go to bed alone and sleep through an eclipse or just be in bed.

This sounds like grandma's advice but it has a scientific basis. Time is increasingly proving that much of grandma's traditional advice has a scientific basis. During some of the solar eclipses, there may be harmful cosmic rays in the atmosphere, which is why scientists ask you not to see it directly but through dark glasses or through a reflection in the water. It is, therefore, best for pregnant women to keep away from sunlight and not watch an eclipse. This will protect her from harmful effects of the sun.

It is safest, therefore, for pregnant women to sleep through eclipses.

Q35. **Is it safe to drive in pregnancy?**

Ans. There is no harm if one is driving carefully when pregnant. Avoid rash driving and bouncing fast over speed breakers. Avoid rush hour traffic if you can. Avoid braking suddenly.

Q36. **Why has my doctor told me to stay away from my cat, and avoid gardening in pregnancy?**

Ans. Toxoplasmosis is a parasitic infection that can be acquired from soil, cat faeces and raw meat. It is an infection present in birds and animals. It is also a common dormant infection in humans, more so in hot and humid climates. If a woman is infected before she becomes pregnant, her baby will not be threatened by it.

To prevent herself from getting infected, a woman can follow some simple guidelines. She should eat only well-cooked meat and eggs and drink only pasteurised or boiled milk. Avoid handling raw meat. When handling raw meat, the hands should be washed immediately and kitchen surfaces and vessels washed well, thereafter. Do not touch the mouth or eyes when handling raw meat. Wash fruits and vegetables before consumption. Protect food from flies and cockroaches. When gardening or handling faeces of animals, use gloves.

The woman who catches this infection in pregnancy has a fifty percent chance of passing it to the baby. If the infection is identified and treated with antibiotics (spiramycin, for instance), it reduces the risk of damage to the baby by fifty to sixty percent. Infection can result mainly in abnormalities of the brain and growth retardation.

Q37. Can I have medicines?

Ans. It is best not to have medicines when pregnant. However, at times one cannot avoid having medicines even though one is pregnant. Some of the instances when having medicines becomes necessary is if one has a urinary tract infection, high blood pressure or premature contractions.

Q38. Should one wear heels in pregnancy?

Ans. Walking with heels alters the centre of gravity of one's body. Pregnancy also alters the centre of gravity of a woman's body because of the extra weight on the front of the body. It is, therefore, best to avoid heels. Wearing heels can increase one's chances of falling and also of backache.

Q39. Can I chew tobacco in pregnancy?

Ans. It is best not to chew tobacco in pregnancy at all. Nicotine, a drug present in tobacco gets secreted in the breast milk, saliva and urine. Tobacco consumption in pregnancy is associated with an increased loss of male foetuses, low birth weight of the baby and an increased risk of stillbirths. Tobacco is also known to cause cancer in healthy human beings, so it is to be generally avoided.

Q40. Can one travel by air in pregnancy?

Ans. If you have high blood pressure or if you have had a miscarriage or bleeding at the beginning of your pregnancy, travelling by air, even in late pregnancy, is not advisable since the change in altitude may cause premature labour.

Flying in an unpressurised aircraft during the first three months of pregnancy can cause serious oxygen deprivation to the baby. However, all modern passenger aircraft are properly pressurised.

If travelling across time zones, even in a perfectly normal pregnancy, avoid travelling during the last six weeks of pregnancy.

Q41. What about dancing in pregnancy?

Ans. Any activity that you are used to normally can be continued in pregnancy, be it dancing, climbing stairs, jogging, etc.

Q42. Is swimming supposed to be good?

Ans. Swimming is an excellent form of exercise that can be continued through pregnancy. All you need is a clean swimming pool and a swimming costume that fits!

Q43. How risky are mobile phones and computers for pregnant women?

Ans. Mobile phones are not meant to be good for anybody. They are said to give out radiation to the head region when in use. Various studies have been done on the effect of computers on pregnant women but

nothing conclusive has come out so far. Earlier, it was considered that the computer screens gave out harmful radiation. However, recent studies have shown that the area behind the computer has greater radiation.

Q44. What type of food should be avoided during pregnancy?

Ans.   All food that comes out of cans or packets is best avoided. Unseasonal food is avoidable. Food products that are highly refined, e.g. *maida* and sugar-based products are avoidable. Alcohol is to be avoided. Food with *ajinomoto*, that is, mono sodium glutamate, mostly present in soup powders, chips, and Chinese cuisine, is also not advisable.

Also avoid strong tea, coffee, colas and chocolates. The stronger they are, more the caffeine in them. Caffeine is a substance that prevents calcium and iron absorption. So, if consumed at all, they are best had between meals when no other food is present for digestion. Between meals, the caffeine will only make you pass more urine which could flush out vitamins B and C with it.

Food with excessive salt like pickles, *papads*, sardines, ham, bacon, dried fish are to be avoided.

Q45. When should a working woman ideally take leave when she is pregnant?

Ans. If a woman is comfortable at work in spite of her pregnancy, she can work till as late as possible and take most of her leave after the birth of the baby.

Q46. When does a mother start feeling the baby's movements?

Ans. Approximately around four to six months of pregnancy.

Q47. How many movements should there be?

Ans. Ten movements, big and small, in twelve hours indicate that all is well. If you feel very concerned and want to know immediately if all is well, you can try this. Sit down quietly and be still. Then eat something. It will probably result in a movement. You need to be still and quiet so that you do not miss the movement, as can happen if you are busy with some activity.

It is best not to get overly worried or paranoid about movements. The baby, like us, can have periods of long sleep which should not be a thing to worry about. For instance, don't we wake up early some days and late on others, sleep soundly sometimes and fitfully at other times?

Q48. How to count them?

Ans.   To count movements, choose a time of least activity. Say 3 pm onwards, you need to count ten movements in twelve hours, or, let us half it, and say five movements in six hours. So, 3 pm to 9 pm would be six hours. Sit down quietly and start counting the movements. Suppose you have counted five movements by 6 pm, you need not carry on counting. The moment you reach the optimum number, be it six, seven or eight o'clock, you can stop counting.

Q49. What if the movements suddenly stop?

Ans.   If you feel no movement in the six hour period, call your doctor. Also, if you feel less than five movements in six hours, call your doctor.

If you are going overdue, that is, from the day you cross your estimated date of delivery, you can start noting down the movements at the same time every day. You can stop counting after the fifth movement. This is a simple way by which you can keep a tab on the baby's well-being.

Q50. What are premature babies?

Ans. Premature babies are babies that are born before they are due to be born. Babies born two weeks before the estimated dated of delivery are not considered premature.

If a premature baby is born with a very low birth weight, it could need special care in a special nursery.

Q51. If I do not wish to retain my pregnancy, can I have medicine to end it?

Ans. Recently the government has approved of a medicine for abortion. It is not available over the counter at chemist shops. It is available with gynaecologists. It has to be taken within forty-nine days or seven weeks of pregnancy, that is, about nineteen to twenty days after a missed period. Before the medicine is given, the doctor will check and rule out an ectopic pregnancy. The medicine is made up of two drugs; one is an anti-pregnancy (anti-progesterone) drug and the other is an expulsive drug (prostoglandin). After it is given, bleeding starts and can continue for seven to ten days. After the bleeding stops, an ultrasound is done to make sure the abortion is complete. In case of an incomplete abortion, a minor operation (D&C) will be performed. This medicine, therefore, can be had only where medical support and backup are available. It has a ninety-five percent success rate. In five percent of cases when it fails, it has to be backed up by a D&C.

Q52. **What is the maximum number of abortions a woman can have?**

Ans. The best way to avoid pregnancy is through contraception. Consult a good gynaecologist, family planning clinic or health centre.

Abortion should not be seen as a method of contraception. It could cause an infection, and require treatment by antibiotics. Frequent or many abortions could lead to pelvic inflammatory disease or sometimes, infertility. Besides, a woman can often find an abortion emotionally and psychologically traumatic.

Q53. **When is an abortion recommended?**

Ans. Medically, an abortion may be offered if there is a family history of chromosomal problems, that is, a genetic counsellor may find that a child carries an abnormality and may advise to terminate the pregnancy.

Victims of rape are also offered an abortion. Sometimes abortion naturally occurs in pregnancy. It could happen in one-third of all first pregnancies. When a miscarriage occurs spontaneously, it could be medically called threatened, repeated or incomplete abortion.

Q54. If you sit cross-legged on the floor, does it flatten the baby's head?

Ans. The best thing you can do is to sit cross-legged as this exercises the pelvic joints, the very joints that 'open up' during the birth of the baby.

With regular exercise, the joints become flexible and open easily at birth. Little wonder, sweeperwomen deliver easily. The baby is safely ensconced in the womb and gets no direct pressure on its head.

Q55. I feel very itchy over my abdomen since I am pregnant. I also have a rash of red blotches now.

Ans. Some pregnant women develop an itchy skin and find red bumps appearing on the abdomen and breasts. This is due to stretching of the skin and can be aggravated by heavy perspiration or stress. For temporary relief, try an oil massage, or gently rub a soft cotton cloth on your abdomen. Calamine lotion may have a soothing effect. Having a bath with sodabicarb (1 tablespoon in a big bucket) added to the bath water can give temporary relief. Bach Flower remedies can also help. These remedies are available in well-stocked homeopathic pharmacies. The flower remedy called Crab Apple can also be applied on the itchy skin. Take any moisturiser on your palm, mix it with three drops of Crab Apple and apply on your abdomen. Reapply as required.

Q56. I am five months pregnant and hardly show. Why is that?

Ans. Some pregnant women who have been athletes, dancers or those who have been exercising regularly and are tall, do not show much. This is because they have a strong set of healthy muscles. It does not mean that something is wrong with the baby.

Q57. Ever since I got pregnant, my nose feels itchy and I have a cold. Is it related?

Ans. Mucous membranes inside the nose and sinuses often swell up during pregnancy on account of certain hormones that also soften up the vagina and mouth of the womb in preparation for birth. Some women, therefore, develop a permanent cold in late pregnancy. However, this will not interfere with your ability to do breathing exercises during labour.

Q58. I get a feeling of pins and needles in the fingers in the morning since my pregnancy. Why?

Ans. Tingling and numbness may be felt in the hands in the morning due to pressure on the nerves and tendons by the accumulated fluid in the hands and wrist. It is felt more in the morning when your wrists have accumulated fluid during the night. To relieve the discomfort, hold your hands above your head for a few minutes and point your fingers towards the ceiling, and open and close fists alternatively. Try and control the swelling in your body by reducing salt in the diet.

Q59. If I develop high fever in pregnancy, can I take antibiotics? Will they harm the baby?

Ans. Avoid taking medicines on your own. Whatever medicine you take should only be under your doctor's advice. Indiscriminate use of certain medicines or drugs can harm the baby. It is best to keep drug intake to the minimum.

Q60. If I have thyroid, should I conceive?

Ans. You will need to see a doctor and have your thyroid treated first. The doctor will bring your condition under control before he allows you to get pregnant.

Q61. What is the cause for varicose veins in pregnancy?

Ans. Varicose veins are dark looking veins that are swollen and might appear on the legs during pregnancy and sometimes remain thereafter.

Veins are blood vessels that carry impure blood to the heart for purification. In pregnancy, hormones cause the veins to relax and hence reduce their efficiency. This causes impure blood to pool in the legs, causing varicose veins to appear. To prevent their appearance, avoid standing for long periods without moving. Do not cross your legs when sitting on a chair, since the weight of one leg over the other for a long time reduces circulation in the legs. Put your feet up on a stool whenever possible. When sitting on a chair, place your feet on a table, or when lying on the floor, place feet on a chair or a bed. Do this, at least once a day for five to ten minutes.

Q62. Is a test for venereal diseases compulsory?

Ans. It is important to test for venereal diseases. Both partners should have the test. If there is a venereal infection, treatment by medicines is important because left untreated, venereal diseases can harm the baby.

Q63. What is toxemia?

Ans. Toxemia is a condition that can cause harm to the unborn baby if it progresses unchecked. When unchecked, it can cause the placenta to fail, and premature labour.

Toxemia usually occurs only during the last few weeks of pregnancy and has three typical symptoms. Any of these symptoms, appearing by itself, does not spell toxemia. It is only when they appear together that a person has toxemia. The three symptoms are:

1. raised blood pressure,
2. swelling of hands, feet and face, and
3. appearance of protein in the urine.

A well-balanced diet with more protein and less carbohydrates and salt reduces the incidence of toxemia. Rest also helps. If symptoms continue, the woman is admitted to the hospital for monitoring and/or treatment. Sometimes the baby might be delivered early, since once the woman starts excreting a high proportion of protein in her urine, the pregnancy is not likely to continue for longer than two weeks.

Danger signs are headaches and flashing lights and sometimes, nausea, vomiting and pain in the abdomen.

Q64. I have a urine infection.

Ans. A urine infection should be treated by the doctor. Left untreated, the infection can travel up to the kidney. The doctor will prescribe a course of antibiotics. There are some things you can do at home to prevent the infection from getting worse and relieving it. You can also do these things if you tend to frequently suffer from urine infection.

1. Drink plenty of water or other liquids like a lemon barley drink, *lassi*, tea, etc. Try and drink something every half an hour so that the strength of the urine gets diluted and the infection gets flushed out.

2.   This infection is easily caused in women because of the female anatomy, since the urethra, vaginal opening and anus are very close to one another. Germs from the stool get transmitted very easily to the urethra and vagina. To reduce the infection, every time you pass a stool, wash the anal area not only with water but with soap and water. Do not bring your hand forward towards the urinary opening as you do so. During your bath, wash the anal area with soap and water separately.

Q65. I pass wind very often and it is very embarrassing.

Ans.   Flatulence, or wind, is not harmful but embarrassing. Try keeping away from company when you are passing wind. Avoid gaseous food like beans, peas, rich food and excessive amounts of greens.

Q66. I have a killing pain below my breasts.

Ans.   Pain under the breasts or just below the ribs is common as pregnancy advances, say after the sixth month. The reason is that as the baby grows, it extends upwards to below the breasts and tends to push up your organs like the liver, stomach, etc., towards the chest cavity. You will find that stretching your arms up, straight above your head, helps relieve discomfort, since it lifts the rib cage off the growing uterus. Also, sitting straight rather than slouching forward will be more comfortable.

Q67. Why can't I sleep at night?

Ans. Stress and worry can cause it. If you are worried about your pregnancy or approaching birth, discuss it with your spouse or doctor. It is likely that once you have voiced them, the worries will disappear.

At times, although sleep comes to you when you retire to bed at night, you may be woken up in a few hours by a desire to pass urine, or by the baby kicking. Thereafter, it may be difficult to go back tosleep. Restrict your fluid intake at night or late in the evening. Try not to worry too much about not being able to go back to sleep. Recite a prayer or a poem in your mind, or your favourite song. Avoid coffee in the evening as it is a mild stimulant and might keep you awake at night. A hot cup of milk just before retiring to bed will help you to relax. A warm salt water bath is also relaxing. Try and consciously relax by doing some deep breathing or the yogic *shavasana*, the corpse pose.

If you sleep in the afternoon, it would help if you stopped it so that you can sleep better at night. Instead of a nap in the afternoon, you could just relax for about half an hour with music or a book, putting your feet up as you do so.

Q68. **I am told I should have taken a Hepatitis B injection before conceiving.**

Ans. A Hepatitis B injection before conceiving will prevent an attack of Hepatitis B in pregnancy, which is good. If you are already pregnant and have not taken the injection, just be careful that you eat clean food and drink safe water.

If the mother already has Hepatitis B, there is a ninety percent chance that she will pass it to her baby. If a mother testifies to having Hepatitis B, the baby needs to be vaccinated at birth with the first dose. The second dose should be given a month later and the third, six months later.

Q69. **Why do I feel dizzy sometimes, as though I am going to faint?**

Ans. Because of lowering of blood pressure, not enough oxygen reaches the brain. Sometimes this causes fainting or dizziness. Dizzy spells may also be caused by anaemia.

In the first three months of pregnancy, the blood pressure is lower than normal. This is why some women complain of dizziness when they first become pregnant. Some of them might actually lose consciousness for a moment or two. This is not harmful to the baby or the mother, except that the mother might injure herself if she falls to the ground in a faint.

In case you have a tendency towards dizzy spells or fainting, avoid crowded and smoky atmosphere and long journeys. Avoid moving too suddenly from a lying or sitting position.

Q70. My stomach feels bloated. I often feel nauseous and suffer from acidity.

Ans. Try and make sure your stomach is never hundred percent empty, nor hundred percent full, that is, keep eating a little throughout the day.

For instance, between breakfast and lunch, eat a sandwich or a banana. Avoid long gaps between lunch, tea and dinner.

Keep a snack that you can easily digest by your bedside at night, and eat it before day break. For instance you could keep biscuits, cake or a sandwich, and eat when you get up in the middle of the night.

Do not worry about the nutritive value of the food. Just eat what you can digest and not vomit out. Marie Gold and cream cracker biscuits are very light and can be digested easily. You could also have cold, boiled potatoes from the fridge, salted for taste.

Q71. I find it difficult to sit continuously on a chair in the office.

Ans.   If you have a desk job, try and make little trips to the desks of your colleagues or to the bathroom. Roll a hand towel and try and place it at the base of your back where the bottom touches the seat.

If you sit back in your chair, you can put the rolled towel in the hollow of your back, at the middle where your back curves a little.

3
Problems

Q72. After how many days of delivery can I start yoga and other exercises?

Ans. In my book *Pregnancy* (Rupa & Co.), in the Chapter 'After Childbirth', there is a list of exercises the mother can do from day one after birth up to six weeks or forty days.

These exercises make you gain a lot of mileage when done at this time because the body is still under the influence of relaxing hormones. These exercises cause the muscles to be repositioned to their prepregnant positions and therefore restore a mother's figure beautifully.

When breastfeeding exclusively, it is difficult to get away from the baby, so these exercises can be continued up to six months. After six months, the mother can do yoga, aerobics, etc. Yoga is the best form of exercise.

It takes around eight to twelve months to regain your figure after childbirth.

Q73. I am pregnant and suffering from chronic constipation. Suggest some remedies.

Ans. *Bhindi* or okra (lady's finger) helps constipation. Eating dried figs (*anjir*) also helps, but the older generation may ask you not to have them because they are too hot. In that case, you can soak them in water overnight and have them in the morning.

Drinking plenty of water and having *Isabgol* will also help constipation. Eating *sabut* or *chilka dal* is also helpful. So is eating fruits without peeling the skin off.

Q74. What are the exercises recommended in pregnancy for backache?

Ans. The simplest exercise for backache in pregnancy is to go into the 'all fours' position, that is, on the hands and knees, just like a dog or a cat. The pregnant woman should remain like that for about three to five minutes, without hollowing her back.

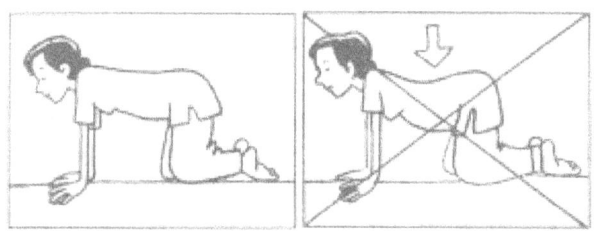

Q75. I have a very busy schedule in the office. Before lunch time, I start feeling very hungry, sluggish and lethargic. How can I overcome this problem?

Ans. Around 11 am or 12 noon, try and eat or drink something. You could have any of these: Sweet *lassi, channa,* banana, fresh fruit juice, any seasonal fruit, a cheese cube, raw nuts, e.g. cashew nuts, almonds, etc., *nimbupani,* milk.

Q76. I am anaemic.

Ans. You can improve your haemoglobin by eating the right things. You need to eat coriander (*dhania*), mint (*pudina*), raddish leaves (*mooli patta*), raisins (*kishmish*), cauliflower leaves (*phool gobi patta*), soya bean, etc.

However, when you eat all this, do not have tea, coffee, cola or chocolates along with them because they contain caffeine which will block iron absorption.

Nimbupani is good because vitamin C in lemons aids iron absorption. You could squeeze a lemon in your salad too.

Avoid taking iron tablets with your meals. Have them with a biscuit between meals. Let the digestive system tackle natural iron from the food and synthetic iron from tablets, one at a time. Taken together, they might interfere with absorption.

Q77. I am thalassemic minor. How do I improve my haemoglobin level?

Ans. There is no way the haemonglobin level can rise dramatically through your diet. However, it has been observed that some thalassemic women have had their haemoglobin level rise after homeopathic treatment.

Q78. How can putting on extra weight after delivery be controlled?

Ans. When breastfeeding, a mother needs more calories than when she is pregnant. Consequently, she feels very hungry, and may end up eating too much of rich food.

Rich food could mean traditional *ladoos* and *panjiri*, pastries, ice creams, fried food, etc. Among these, *ladoos* and *panjiri* are nutritively superior to ice creams and pastries. They should be eaten in moderation when a period of activity is going to follow. If the mother eats them after meals and then goes to sleep, she will put on a lot of weight. She should eat these before feeding the baby during the day and be active thereafter.

When preparing traditional recipes, calories can be drastically reduced by reducing the *ghee* content. For instance, if you roast the *atta*/flour or *suji*/cream of wheat before making the dish, it will soak in very little *ghee* when cooking.

To avoid putting on too much weight, one can eat salad or a bowl of curd before the main meal so that hunger lessens. Eat the food slowly and chew it well. This aids digestion. Avoid eating calorierich leftover food of your baby.

Eat something at home before going out for a social gathering. You should not have hunger pangs when you go or it will make you reach out for fried snacks.

If you are having milk, try and have it plain, without sugar or any other flavouring.

Q79. I have swollen hands and feet.

Ans. You need to avoid food with a high salt content and carbohydrates or sugar.

Avoid pickles, *papad*, cheese, sardines, ham, salami, bacon, dried fish, salted *namkeens* and salted nuts.

You also need to avoid too much of potatoes, bread, rice, *chapati*, *mathi*, cold drinks or sweet tea, chocolates and puddings.

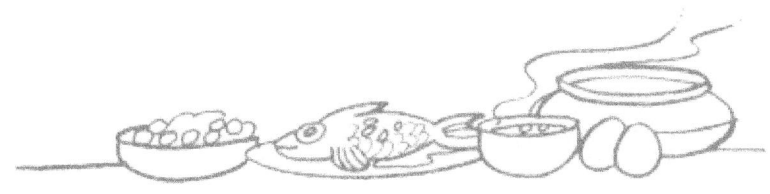

What you need to eat is extra protein, that is, *dal*, curds, *besan*, *channa*, sprouts. So if you eat three to four *chapatis*, reduce one *chapati* and have an extra bowl of *dal* or curd instead. You can also eat eggs, fish, chicken and meat.

Q80. I had stopped smoking during pregnancy. Can I continue to smoke after childbirth?

Ans. It is not advisable to smoke, chew tobacco or drink strong alcohol like whiskey, rum or vodka when breastfeeding the baby.

Q81. I have pain in the groin and sides of my abdomen since the eighth month of pregnancy. Why?

Ans. In late pregnancy, it is common to have pain in the pelvic region since the joints of the pelvic girdle soften in preparation for birth. Avoid standing for a long time. The pain might also result from stretching of the round ligament which holds the uterus in place.

Q82. **I am six months pregnant. While going through a revolving door, I bumped my abdomen against it. Will the baby be hurt?**

Ans. The baby inside the womb is well-protected and lies in a sac of fluid which acts like a shock absorber. Gentle bumps should not be a cause of worry. Yes, strong jerks, a push, a kick or trauma can cause harm to the baby as well as the mother.

Q83. **What if I have tuberculosis or have been on ATT (anti-tuberculosis treatment)?**

Ans. If you have tuberculosis and get pregnant, you will need to continue your medication under the doctor's supervision not only in pregnancy but also during childbirth, breastfeeding and afterwards. Tuberculosis does not require a medical termination per se. Even if you have been on an anti-tuberculosis treatment, you can get pregnant. In active tuberculosis of the lungs, the mother may not be allowed to breastfeed and the baby may be kept away from her.

Q84. **What if I have an inherited abnormality like muscular dystrophy, cystic fibrosis or haemophilia?**

Ans. If you have any such inherited disorder and are planning a baby, consult the genetic counselling unit in a big hospital. They will help reduce your chances of passing on the disorder to your baby.

Once you get pregnant, you will need to go through medical tests to investigate whether your baby is carrying the disorder or not. If the disorder is detected, a termination may be recommended by your doctor.

Q85. **I am diabetic. Is it okay for me to get pregnant?**

Ans. You need to get your diabetes under control before you get pregnant. Once pregnant, you need antenatal supervision every month up to twenty weeks and thereafter, at two week intervals up to thirty weeks. It is best for you to consult a team of experts so that your baby is born at term and healthy, and you have no complications. The experts you need to consult are: 1. Nutritionists; 2. General Physician; 3. Pediatrician; 4. Obstetrician/Gynaecologist.

You will have to be very strict with your diet. It is difficult to stabilise the blood sugar during pregnancy due to altered carbohydrate metabolism and reduced insulin action. It is important to deliver in a big hospital.

Q86. I am a heart patient. Is it alright for me to get pregnant?

Ans. It is okay to get pregnant if you are a heart patient. However, you need to be under the care of a cardiologist, along with your gynaecologist/obstetrician. You need to visit them at an interval of two weeks up to twenty-eight weeks, and thereafter at weekly intervals. In addition to that, you need to maintain a good diet, take adequate rest and avoid excitement. Avoid catching cold and other infections. It is important to deliver in a big, well-equipped hospital.

Q87. Is bleeding gums a common pregnancy-related problem?

Ans. During pregnancy, the gums soften and are therefore more likely to catch infection and start bleeding. Infection in the gums can mean infection in the teeth also, and consequent tooth decay. In order that infection does not set in, it is important to brush your teeth regularly and keep your mouth clean. The good old Indian habit of swishing the mouth a few times with fresh water after a meal is good. That apart, brush before sleeping. In pregnancy, your gums and teeth are in a more delicate condition, so a soft brush is preferred to a hard one. A brush with a small head reaches all corners of your mouth. Change your toothbrush when the bristles begin to look droopy or flat.

Q88. I often get cramps in my legs.

Ans.   Leg cramps mostly occur in the last months of pregnancy and are rather painful. Various factors are believed to cause them such as sluggish blood circulation, lack of calcium, lack of vitamin B, lack of vitamin E. The best way to relieve a cramp is to point the big toe towards the face when it happens. Include in your diet, milk products like curds, green vegetables and whole *dals* so that any deficiency can be taken care of.

If cramps happen at night or in the mornings, walk across a six feet long area on your toes, then on your heels and lastly on the outer sides of your feet. Done everyday before going to bed, it has given relief to a lot of women.

Take extra salt, specially at night, if cramps occur when you are trying to go on a salt-free diet.

Sometimes extreme cold can cause a cramp. If you are sleeping in the draught of an air conditioner, you can focus the draught elsewhere or adjust the air conditioner to a warmer temperature.

Q89. I hear piles is a very common problem in pregnancy.

Ans. In pregnancy, a muscle relaxing hormone called relaxin is secreted by the body which relaxes the digestive tract. Therefore, if constipation stays over a period of time in pregnancy, it can cause veins around the anus to protrude from the strain that accompanies constipation, leading to piles or permanently protruding veins around the anus. To prevent piles, and if piles occur, prevent constipation and avoid spicy food.

Q90. What is the remedy for indigestion and heartburn?

Ans. To prevent indigestion and heartburn, never let your stomach be too full or too empty. Avoid spicy and heavy food, that is, avoid food with rich *masalas*. Do not eat more than one tablespoon of green vegetables at a time. Reduce the amount of raw food with roughage, for instance, tomatoes and apples that have a skin that can irritate the stomach. Boiled potatoes and bananas will soothe the stomach because they do not have roughage.

Q91. I burp very loudly in pregnancy.

Ans. Burping depends entirely on the amount of air a person swallows. If you eat quickly or speak quickly, or swallow a lot of air when you cry, you are likely to burp.

Q92. Should a frequent vaginal discharge worry me?

Ans. It is common to have a non-irritating whitish vaginal discharge. The function of this discharge is to keep the vagina free of infection and clean. If the discharge turns yellow or green and causes itching or burning, get in touch with your doctor.

Q93. Should one eat *ghee* in late pregnancy?

Ans. It is in the ninth month of pregnancy that the baby puts on most of its weight. So eating *ghee* at this time may give the baby a better birth weight.

As such, eating *ghee* or fats in any other form helps in the absorption of fat soluble vitamins A, D, E and K which are essential for a healthy and strong body.

If you eat *ghee* regularly but do not do much work in the house and do not go for regular walks either, it could result in extra weight and stiff joints, making delivery difficult. However, if you are active and are not overweight and do not have any cholesterol problems, you can go ahead and have *ghee*.

One tablespoon of *ghee* is 15 grams. The permitted amount of *ghee* or butter during pregnancy and breastfeeding is 30 to 45 grams a day respectively, according to the National Institute of Nutrition, Hyderabad. Hence, one tablespoon of *ghee* falls within the permissible limit. When you add one tablespoon of *ghee* to your diet in the ninth month of pregnancy, you can cut down on high calorie food such as puddings, chocolates and fried food, etc.

Throughout the day, one could have a tablespoon of pure homemade *ghee* on one's *chapatis* and in *dal*. Some women might prefer to have pure homemade butter on a *paratha* instead. *Ghee* is traditionally had in a hot cup of milk, sweetened as preferred.

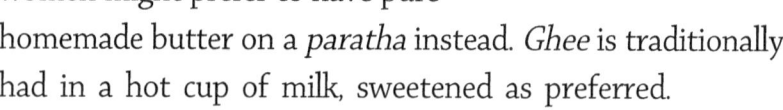

Q94. What is HIV/AIDS?

Ans. A blood test is carried out to detect the Human Immunodeficiency Virus or HIV. A person who tests positive for HIV has a strong possibility of developing AIDS or Acquired Immuno Deficiency Syndrome, in which case, the person's immunity or strength to fight infection falls drastically. The person can then pick up all kinds of infections, i.e. colds, respiratory infections, skin infections, etc. If a woman is suffering from AIDS, she can pass the infection to her newborn baby.

Q95. What happens to a mother who has HIV or AIDS?

Ans. If the mother has HIV infection, pregnancy can increase her chances of developing AIDS.

However, if a woman is known to be HIV or AIDS infected and gets pregnant, recent research has shown that the use of two standard drugs azt and 3tc can prevent the passing of the virus from the mother to the baby.

Recent research also shows that without treatment, eighteen percent of babies can be infected whereas with treatment, the infection of babies can be lowered to eleven percent if the two drugs are given when labour begins, and continued for a week after birth. The medicine can be given to the mother when labour starts. It must be given to both the mother and child for a week following birth. This is to protect the child from exposure to AIDS contaminated blood and secretions as well as from virus in the breast milk which causes one-third of all infections in the young. The risk of infection can be further reduced to nine percent if treatment is begun twenty-six weeks before delivery and continued for a week afterwards.

A new drug called Nevirapine is also known to reduce the transmission of HIV from the mother to the baby, and costs much less than azt. Nevirapine is administered to an HIV infected woman in labour and another dose is given to the baby within three days of birth.

Q96. What is an ultrasound?

Ans. An ultrasound was first used during the Second World War to detect submarines. In an ultrasound, sound waves of an exceedingly high frequency, above

20,000 Hz, that cannot be heard by the human ear, are bounced off structures in order to give a picture of the structure they bounce off from.

In pregnancy, these sound waves are directed to the foetus inside the uterus, and as they bounce off the baby's bones and tissues, a picture of the foetus appears on a TV screen. The bony framework of the baby shows up as white on the TV screen. The fluid-filled areas show up as black.

Q97. How is an ultrasound done?

Ans. When you go for an ultrasound scan, you must have a full bladder. You will be made to lie down next to the machine and a gel will be spread over your abdomen. A small flat device will be moved slowly all over your abdomen during the scan.

Q98. When is an ultrasound done in pregnancy?

Ans. In women receiving infertility treatment, an ultrasound may be done early in pregnancy. In a normal pregnancy, an ultrasound is done between sixteen to twenty weeks. At this time, it gives an accurate idea of how old the pregnancy is. After twenty-four weeks, the baby's age in the uterus cannot be accurately predicted by an ultrasound. Apart from this, an ultrasound may be done if the doctor thinks it is advisable for investigative purposes.

Q99. Is it possible to have no ultrasound in pregnancy?

Ans. Yes, it is possible to have no ultrasound during one's pregnancy.

Q100. How safe is ultrasound?

Ans. It is a fairly new technology and began to be widely used in obstetrics in India only in the late 1970s or early 1980s. In other words, it is in its infancy. It does not appear to harm the mother or the baby in any way but there is no evidence that it is completely safe either. It took forty years to discover the harmful effects of X-ray which was the only technique of getting some information of the baby in the uterus before the ultrasound scan.

Q101. What information can an ultrasound give?

Ans. As a diagnostic tool, the ultrasound is invaluable since it can give the doctor vital information on diagnosis of pregnancy, missed abortion, hydatidiform mole, twin pregnancies, the position of the foetus and placenta, the age of the foetus and abnormalities of the foetus or the uterus. Scans should be done in pregnancy if the doctor thinks it is advisable for investigative purposes. As a routine procedure, it is avoidable. It is best used sparingly.

Most women agree to have the ultrasound done because the professionals advise that it is absolutely safe. Actually, Medical Research Council, UK, had in 1981 considered conducting a trial on the advantages and disadvantages of ultrasound before its use became general. But their proposal was never implemented. They were told that it was likely that any delicate irregularities found could have other causes.

According to Marjorie Tew, in her book *Safer Childbirth?*, 1995, 'It has never been tested whether there is an upper safe limit to the number of scans, though there is now some evidence that birthweight is lower after several scans. Nor is it known whether safety is related to a scan's duration, which can vary widely in length, or to the power of the instrument used, which also varies widely between models, newer models usually being much more powerful that the older ones used in the 1970s'.

Exposure to the baby can be greater with the vaginal ultrasound as it bypasses the protection of the mother's body. Electronic foetal monitors, Doppler monitors and hand-held sonic devices also use ultrasound.

'Studies which showed that ultrasound was safe were done when women were given only one ultrasound scan, in the sixteenth week; after all the major fetal organs had been formed.'

Today, mostly in the urban Indian setting, ultrasound scans in early pregnancy confirm normalcy. However, sometimes in the end, few verdicts may be reversed, resulting in great amounts of stress for the mother. For few women, abnormalities may be incorrectly diagnosed. Some abnormalities, like the position of the placenta, or the presentation of the foetus may be diagnosed at the time of the scan but correct themselves before delivery without any intervention or treatment. However, this again causes undue stress to the mother. It is only in a very small minority of women that an abnormality will be correctly diagnosed and if it is serious, a termination of pregnancy may be suggested.

In her book *Safer Childbirth?*, Tew further says, 'Interpreting ultrasound images obviously requires considerable skill, but there is no recognized training which all operators, who may be general radiographers or doctors or midwives, must take before they practice ...Inevitably there may be variations in the quality and accuracy of the diagnoses they make and on the reliance that can be put on these as bases for further treatment'.

Q102. Why should ultrasound be used sparingly?

Ans. Dr Ian Donald started the use of ultrasound in pregnancy. Forty years later, he wrote that ultrasound should 'never lose its submissiveness to the medical art. Out of control, it can be an obsession, a tail that wags the dog...the possibility of hazard should be kept under constant review'. (*Source:* Association of Improvement in Maternity Services, AIMS, UK, 1994).

Besides, according to scientists at the Indian Institute of Science, Bangalore, when ultrasound waves are passed through a liquid at a particular power and frequency, they creates light emitting bubbles. This would imply that 'use of high intensity ultrasound in medical diagnosis is potentially harmful to the tissues'.

Q103. The ultrasound shows my baby is too big/too small.

Ans. There can be various factors that can lead to this discrepancy.

1. According to medical textbooks, babies can be born two weeks before or two weeks after the estimated date of delivery. Therefore, two weeks earlier will not be considered premature and two weeks later will not be considered post-mature. Hence, a two week variation should not be of much concern.

2. Machines can be influenced by their place of origin in the reading they give. For instance, German babies are born bigger at birth than Japanese babies. A German machine will consider the average birth weight of German babies to compute data of the growing foetus. Likewise, a Japanese machine will consider the average birth weight of a Japanese baby to compute data of the growing foetus. Average Indian babies are born 3 kilograms or 6 pounds in weight. If you are concerned that your baby is too small, you can do the following:

Rest more and lie down. Lie on your side. Do deep breathing in the garden in the morning. Eat high protein foods, *dals*, curds, sprouts, eggs, meat, fish. Eat some butter or *ghee* also.

If you are concerned that your baby is too big, concentrate on eating fruits and go for walks. Avoid fried and sweet food. Remember, the head of the baby has the capacity to mould to the mother's birth canal. The mother's birth canal has the capacity to expand at birth, just like a bud expands into a flower. Some babies are even born with a birth weight of 8 or 9 pounds.

Besides, I am not sure we yet understand the intricate growth spurts the foetus goes through in the uterus.

Q104. How does the doctor know my baby is too small?

Ans. The doctor can know from an ultrasound or an abdominal examination.

The height of the growing uterus gives an idea of the growth of the baby. At three months, the uterus can be felt in the lower abdomen, rising out of the pelvis. At five and a half months, the uterus reaches the height of the navel. At seven and a half months, the uterus will be half way between the navel and the breast bone, or the region below the breasts. In the ninth month, the uterus will reach the area below the breasts.

A few weeks before the delivery, the uterus may drop or lower as the baby's head lowers into the mother's pelvis in preparation for birth.

Q105. Ultrasound shows my placenta is calcified/ matured.

Ans.   Ultrasound is a window to the uterus which was not there earlier. As with other technologies, one learns more as one uses it. It is now understood that most placentas mature towards the end of pregnancy, since, as delivery nears, they are reaching the end of their life span.

According to *Mayes' Midwifery* (1997), 'On the natural surface of the placenta small greyish white patches are often to be seen, particularly on the post-mature placenta. These are deposits of lime salts. They convey a gritty sensation to the fingers and are not of any significance'.

Q106. Ultrasound shows the cord is around the baby's neck.

Ans.   Babies are often born with the cord wrapped loosely around their necks. The delivery can be normal.

According to the book *Obstetrics Illustrated* (Churchill Livingstone), 'one or two loops of cord are quite often seen around the baby's neck at vertex delivery and normally do no harm'. One rarely finds six or seven loops around the baby's neck. These could be a cause for concern.

Q107. I have developed diabetes in pregnancy.

Ans.   Some women may develop diabetes in pregnancy while others may be diabetic to begin with.

Diabetes that starts in pregnancy is called gestational diabetes, and is more likely to occur in the last three months of pregnancy. A high glucose level in early pregnancy could mean that the mother was diabetic before pregnancy without realising it. Most women who develop gestational diabetes will find that their glucose level returns to normal after delivery. However, gestational diabetes could return with the next pregnancy. The possibility could be reduced by following a healthy diet and not putting on too much weight.

Pregnant women may frequently show glucose in their urine without having diabetes because in pregnancy, the level at which the glucose spills into the urine from the blood is lowered. A glucose tolerance test can identify whether the woman has an unusually low renal threshold or whether she has diabetes.

Q108. What is natural childbirth?

Ans. As mentioned in the book *Natural Childbirth* by Beatrice Faust (1982, Rigby Publishers, Australia), 'Basically, you need to decide whether you want your baby's birth to be controlled by natural rhythms, which is best for a baby and for you, or by medical routine, which is best for doctors. The natural method is obviously preferable but is not widely accepted yet. Not all doctors, nurses, or hospitals really believe in it. So, if you want it you must be prepared to beg, plead, cajole, persuade, argue, insist and fight for it'.

Q109. How safe is natural childbirth?

Ans. Natural childbirth is quite safe if you are usually in good health. In pregnancy, thirty percent of women may develop a problem that needs a doctor's attention. However, in most cases, women can give birth without drugs or instruments.

Being well-prepared in pregnancy and childbirth helps as one requires less of drugs during childbirth. According to Dr M. Wagner, consultant to WHO on women and child health, 'around ninety per cent of births, if reasonably managed, turn out to be normal'.

Dr R.A. Bradley, author of the book *Husband—Coached Childbirth*, compares childbirth to swimming. He says, 'The doctor is the lifeguard. Both swimming and childbirth carry an irreducible minimal risk and lifeguards and doctors are necessary, but only for complications'.

Q110. Is the estimated date of delivery (EDD) the date on which the baby will be born?

Ans. The estimated date of delivery is not the date of appointment. It is simply the date arrived at by a rough calculation to estimate the average duration of pregnancy. A pregnancy might exceed it or

terminate before it. Studies show that only five percent of babies arrive on the estimated date of delivery.

On an average, a pregnancy lasts two hundred and eighty days, or forty weeks, or nine months and seven days, after the first day of the last menstrual period. There is no disadvantage to the baby if the birth takes place any time between thirty-eight to forty-two weeks of pregnancy.

Q111. How can I calculate my estimated date of delivery?

Ans. To calculate a woman's estimated date of delivery, one takes into account the last menstrual period before her pregnancy. Suppose it began on March 25, one would count seven days ahead and arrive at April 1. Then one would count backwards 3 months, that is March 1, February 1, January 1. This is the shortcut to counting two hundred and eighty days from a fixed date.

4
Labour and After

Q112. Is labour very painful?

Ans.   In case of unbearable pain, nature's safety mechanism makes one pass out, i.e. lose consciousness. In labour, a woman is rendered unconscious by drugs but never by pain. The right attitude to contractions can make it pretty easy to bear.

Q113. What is the drip?

Ans.   The drip implies that glucose/saline drips from a bottle through a tube, straight into your vein, through a needle that is inserted on the back of your hand. The bottle of glucose/saline is attached sometimes to a rod at the side of the bed; and sometimes to a rod attached to a stand with wheels. It prevents dehydration in the mother and gives her energy.

The glucose drip can be used to trigger off labour, when an artificial form of oxytocin hormone (oxytocin is a hormone that causes the uterus to contract), called syntocin, is added to a bottle of glucose/ saline solution and introduced straight into the mother's bloodstream.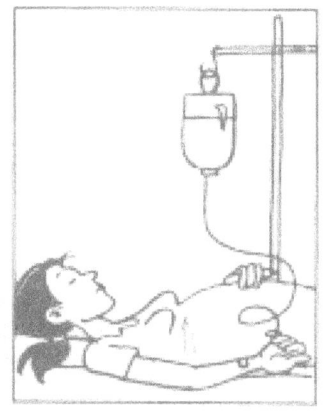

In natural childbirth, oxytocin is secreted by the mother's pituitary gland and makes the uterus have a contraction. This is preferred because when oxytocin is released by the mother's brain, it causes mothering behaviour in the mother and bonding behaviour in the child. The synthetic form of oxytocin, that is, syntocin only works at the physical level and causes unnaturally strong contractions to happen. It has no effect otherwise.

Q114. Does everyone get the drip in labour?

Ans.   No, everyone need not get the drip. One can have the baby without the drip. The drip may be useful in case labour is too long and/or slowing down, or if the mother has high blood pressure. On the other hand, a plain drip may be fixed to prevent dehydration in the mother. However, dehydration can also be prevented if the mother is allowed to eat and drink in labour. She can drink water or water with glucose or honey. She can eat carbohydrates like glucose biscuits, *mishri*, bananas, a jam sandwich without butter. She should not consume fats or proteins, e.g. milk, nuts, *ghee*, etc.

Q115. What are the disadvantages of the drip in labour?

Ans.   Since the drip in labour results in stronger contractions at shorter intervals than natural labour, it reduces oxygen available to the baby by shortening the recovery interval between contractions that the baby has.

(During a contraction, a baby is partially deprived of blood and oxygen. It is between contractions that blood and oxygen reach the baby.)

Though doctors may not always agree that it is more painful than natural labour, they would agree that there is more need for pain relief in induced labour.

Since all pain relieving drugs affect the baby, unnecessary induction should be avoided. Also, due to a combination of oxytocin induction by the drip and drugs, new born babies can be sleepy at birth after an induced labour. They are also more likely to get jaundice.

It was for these reasons that the Lancet, 2 (1977), 467-9, in an editorial on induced labour said, it is a 'wholesale interference with this delicately balanced physiological process', that is labour.

Q116. How will I know that labour has begun?

Ans. Labour may begin in either of the three ways mentioned below, or two of the following may appear together.

1.   A week or more before labour begins, you may notice a thick mucus discharge which could be white, pink or brown in colour. Sometimes it may even have some bright red blood mixed in it. The discharge occurs from the mouth of the womb, which is plugged with mucus to prevent infection from entering the womb.

2.   Pain may be felt periodically, at intervals. When you realise this, begin to make a note of the time whenever the discomfort occurs. If you find it occurs half hourly, you know it is real labour. It could also occur more frequently, for example, every fifteen minutes.

    Sometimes, before labour begins, you feel practice contractions or false contractions. These are contractions of the uterus in preparation for birth. Practice contractions feel similar to real contractions but they occur at irregular intervals, for instance, they can happen after five minutes, then after forty-five minutes, followed by fifteen or thirty minutes, etc.

    So, while practice contractions have a haphazard interval between them, real contractions have fixed rhythmical intervals.

    It is possible that real labour can start and then stop for a day or so. You can safely stay home until your contractions are ten minutes apart. Once they are coming every ten minutes, they are properly established and less likely to stop.

3.   The baby is encased in a bag of water called the amniotic sac. Sometimes this bag bursts and all the water (about one litre) escapes.

    On some occasions, the amniotic sac may not burst but might just trickle instead. The trickle will be clear and uncontrollable. You can wear a sanitary pad and stay at home. After sometime, the sac might seal itself and the trickle might stop.

Q117. When do I go to hospital?

Ans. You go to the hospital if:

- You have ten minute apart contractions. If contractions surprise you and start at five minute intervals, do not panic but go to the hospital.
- If you experience bright, fresh, red, bleeding, without mucus, you need to see the doctor. Occasionally, a few drops of blood may escape a couple of days after intercourse or a vaginal examination by the doctor. This is quite harmless.
- If the trickle of water that escapes from the amniotic sac is not clear, but appears muddy or greenish and/ or has a foul smell, contact your doctor.
- If your water bag bursts, you should go to the hospital, and many hospitals may routinely fix a drip, with a hormone added to it, to stimulate labour.

However, with or without the drip, after the water bag has burst, labour may take four, six or eight hours to start. Hence, there is no harm if you request for the drip to be put off for the first four to five hours in hospital. When you wait, it gives your body the time to naturally release oxytocin hormone (see Q 111).

Q118. How long will labour be?

Ans. Labour has no time limit, time table or time frame. The duration of labour is different in each woman, and also in the same woman during two different deliveries. It is difficult to preplan labour or the duration of labour. You just let it happen in its own time. Very broadly, from the time you start showing the symptoms at home, give yourself approximately twenty-four hours, or more or less than twenty-four hours.

Q119. Does cutting the umbilical cord hurt the mother or the baby?

Ans. Cutting the umbilical cord hurts neither the mother nor the baby.

Q120. Should one delay cutting the umbilical cord?

Ans. According to Dr R.D. Laing, when the baby is born, the umbilical cord is wet and pulsating. It is full of blood which is reaching the baby through it from the placenta. As soon as the baby is born, the doctor clamps the cord and cuts it. It takes approximately five minutes for the baby's own blood circulation to establish. If the cord is not cut immediately, it gives the baby oxygen when this transition is being made. The blood vessels carrying blood from the cord seal off as the baby's own system of circulation takes over. So, if the cord is cut after the newborn's own circulation has taken over, the newborn's adjustment to breathing will be smoother and gentler. However, delaying the cutting of the umbilical cord is not recommended if the stem cells from the umbilical cord are to be harvested.

Q121. Why does the placenta come out after the baby and not with it?

Ans. A contraction expels the placenta after the baby is born. During birth, the placenta carries on its function of supplying blood and oxygen to the baby. Its function is complete after the baby is delivered. Once its function is complete, it is also delivered.

Q122. Is the umbilical cord attached to the mother's navel?

Ans. The umbilical cord is attached to the organ inside the womb called the placenta. This organ prepares and passes food and nutrition to the baby through the umbilical cord, which on the other end is attached to the baby's navel.

Q123. Should you push when in labour?

Ans. When in labour, never push until the doctor or the nurse asks you to. If you begin to push when the mouth of the womb is not fully dilated or open, there is the danger of the baby's head hitting against an unopened cervix (mouth of womb), so that the baby's head and cervix become swollen and tender.

Q124. Is it true that you should walk when in labour?

Ans. The best thing you can do is to walk when in labour. Gravity hastens the baby's decline, and therefore shortens labour. Also, when you lie on your back, the weight of your baby and uterus press on a major blood vessel called the vena cava, hence reducing the supply of blood to you and your baby. Less pain is felt when a woman walks in labour. (*Note:* Labour can begin in various ways. If labour begins with the water bag bursting and a big sudden gush of water, walk only if your doctor permits you to.)

Q125. Does the baby get suffocated if you pull in the stomach?

Ans. The baby does not suffocate, since it gets oxygen through the umbilical cord which is attached to its navel and to the placenta on the other end. If you pull in your stomach, the weight of the baby is borne by the pelvic bones so that your stomach muscles get a respite from constant stretching.

Q126. Should you bind the abdomen after delivery?

Ans. If you make a jumble of your clothes and fling them in your cupboard, they'll fall on your face when you open it next. If you push your muscles back with a girdle, they'll flop out again. It is important to tone your muscles with exercise instead.

Q127. Does coughing and sneezing induce labour?

Ans. It is an uncomfortable feeling but it does not induce labour.

Q128. What is a caesarean section and how is it done?

Ans. If, due to some circumstances, a baby cannot be delivered normally, a surgical extraction is done from the womb. It could be done under epidural or general anaesthesia. An incision is made on the abdomen, often just above the pubic mound, and the baby is manually removed. The incision is then stitched back. Earlier, the incision used to be made from the navel, all the way to the pubic mound.

Q129. Does the vagina remain tight if one goes for a caesarean?

Ans. The vagina prepares for a normal delivery anyway by getting relaxed and loose. Even if you have had a caesarean, you will need to do pelvic floor exercises to regain the prepregnant tightness in the vagina.

Q130. If the baby is in breech presentation, will it be a caesarean?

Ans. If the baby is in breech in early pregnancy, it is likely to turn to a head down position a few weeks before the birth. If it does not turn to a head down position in a woman having her first delivery, a caesarean will be performed. Homeopathic medicine taken from a classical homeopath, one month before the estimated date of delivery, could turn around a breech baby. Also, acupressure point B67 at the base of the little toe nail is known to turn around a breech baby.

Q131. When are you taken up for a caesarean?

Ans.   Indications for a caesarean are:

1.   The umbilical cord is swept down and gets pressed between the baby's head and the mother's pelvic bone. This is possible only if the baby's head does not fix or engage in late pregnancy, and the mother's water bag bursts, so that all the water gushes out.

2.   If the placenta lies in front of the mouth of the womb.

3.   If the placenta separates, causing bright red bleeding.

4.   If the baby is in a feet down position (breech), WHO recommends that if one waits till labour begins, the baby may turn to a head down position. Midwives deliver breech babies normally.

5.   If the baby's head and the pelvic brim or inlet do not fit or align to allow the baby's head to pass through the mother's pelvic bone (cephalopelvic disproportion).

6.   In case of foetal distress—when the baby's heart rate dips below 110 or accelerates above 160 beats per minute. Sometimes a brief discordance is corrected soon. If the mother is lying flat on her back when foetal distress happens, the heart beat will correct itself once she is made to sit or stand up. The position of lying flat on her back compresses the vena cava, a major blood vessel between the pregnant uterus and the mother's back bone, thus reducing the blood flow. It is for this reason that the Royal College of Obstetricians recommended that the mother should not be on the foetal monitor for more than twenty minutes at a time, since being on it requires her to lie flat on her back. It has been known to cause foetal distress.

Q132. If the first child is a caesarean, does the second child have to be a caesarean?

Ans. If it is a recurring factor like a basic fault in the mother's bony pelvic structure, yes, a caesarean will need to be done. But if it is a non-recurring factor like the baby's heart going into distress or a breech presentation at birth, a caesarean does not have to be done for the next baby. However, after two caesareans, the third is, generally, also a caesarean.

Q133. What is induced labour?

Ans.   Induced labour is a way of artificially stimulating the uterus into labour contractions or pains, with the intention of bringing about the birth of the baby.

Q134. What is a forceps delivery?

Ans.   A baby is delivered by forceps at birth if the mother or baby are too tired to push or if the mother suffers from severe pre-eclampsia, high blood pressure or heart disease.

In a forceps delivery, the mother lies on her back with legs supported by stirrups. The forceps look roughly like two circular handles of a scissor or salad spoons with holes in them. These two blades of the forceps are inserted into the vagina and positioned on either side of the baby's head. When the mother gets a contraction, the doctor holds the handle of the forceps and pulls the baby out.

Q135. What is a vacuum delivery?

Ans.   A baby can also be delivered by vacuum extraction at birth. Like forceps, it aids the birth of the baby.

During delivery by vacuum extraction, a cup made of metal or soft material like silicone or rubber is applied on the baby's head, using suction. When the mother gets a contraction, traction or a pull is applied to enhance the mother's expulsive efforts.

Q136. How safe is prolonged pregnancy?

Ans. If labour does not start by approximately two weeks after the estimated date of delivery, the placenta (the organ that nourishes the baby) may start to get less efficient in supporting the baby inside the uterus. This could deprive the baby of nourishment and the doctor may decide to have the baby delivered.

However, many babies who are thought to be overdue are often not born post-mature at all.

A post-mature baby is born typically with a wrinkled look because, as the placental nourishment reduces, it begins to use up its fat reserves to nourish itself. The wrinkles disappear as the baby gains weight after its birth.

Q137. What is cervi-gel?

Ans. It is a gel which contains the hormone prostaglandin. When labour needs to be induced, it may be applied through the vagina, and as it melts, it bathes the cervix and causes labour to begin. Hormones can also be administered to the mother orally through the mouth to induce labour.

Q138. Can I get pregnant if I am pregnant already? That is, if I have sex when I am pregnant, will I get twins?

Ans. No, you cannot get pregnant if you are already pregnant as that pregnancy is secure. All the extra sperms will get wasted.

Q139. Is it common to have mood swings after the birth of the baby?

Ans. Mild mood swings are normal but if a woman is extremely depressed, it is called post-partum depression. Such a woman will cry easily, sleep with difficulty, be tired and irritable, experience fear or inadequacy.

Depression may also creep in when you recall the kind of birth experience you have had or if you are overburdened with work and have no help. Discuss these feelings with a trusted friend and do not bottle up these negative emotions. Take things easy and do not worry too much about dusting not being done, meals not cooked, etc.

If depression persists, you could consult a sympathetic

family physician/homeopathic doctor/psychotherapist. In my experience, most women have responded the fastest and best to homoeopathic medicines. Depression can occur in a perfectly healthy woman. It may be caused due to sudden withdrawal of hormones from the body after the birth of the baby. The doctor may prescribe some hormones, the dose of which will be tapered off. According to *Mayes' Midwifery*, 'The elimination of all sugars from the diet will enable the hormones to rebalance themselves and nutrition therapists also suggest taking supplements of Vitamin B6 and zinc'.

Q140. Is there anything else one can do to prevent depression?

Ans. A flower remedy available at homoeopathic stores called Rescue Remedy can be had (eight drops, four times a day in water). If the mother is tired, a flower remedy called Olive can be had. If the mother is feeling sad about her figure and messy about breastfeeding and baby care, Crab Apple can be had. Rescue/Olive/Crab Apple can be had together if they match the mother's symptoms. They can be had in water, soup, *lassi*, anything. You don't have to be on an empty stomach. Have them for fifteen days.

Q141. How soon after the delivery can you start going out? What is 'forty days' all about?

Ans.   Immediately after childbirth, the muscles are still under the influence of relaxing hormones. Avoid strenuous work for the first forty days. Get extra help for this period so that you can rest and take it easy. If you can, shift to your mother's or mother-in-law's place where you can be taken care of, and your entire focus should be on taking care of the baby. Wherever you are, it is best to be in a room next to the kitchen and avoid steps.

Q142. Is there a cure for stretch marks?

Ans.   Stretch marks are usually inevitable. Many women believe that oiling the skin with vitamin E oil helps. There is no harm in a gentle massage of the stretched abdomen. It is very relieving. If you are lucky, you may find that the marks do not appear at all. A local midwife suggests this recipe for stretchmarks:

1 cup neem leaves
½ cup *sarson* seeds
1 level tsp *haldi* powder
½ tsp salt

Grind into a paste and apply on the mother's abdomen three days after the delivery.

Expose to sunlight or the light of a bedside lamp for ten to fifteen minutes before bath. Continue daily application for six weeks.

Q143. When does a miscarriage happen?

Ans. It happens if the baby is not viable and not likely to survive anyway. It is nature's way of natural selection. Sometimes normal healthy babies miscarry in case of a trauma to the mother, physically or emotionally. A previous history of miscarriage, an abnormal shaped uterus, illness in the mother, low lying placenta, etc. could be other causes of miscarriage. Medical care and bed rest can avoid a miscarriage when it is imminent.

Q144. Is it good for the mother and baby to have a massage after the delivery?

Ans. A massage is a static exercise that enhances blood circulation. It feels wonderful to a mother who can be exhausted from breastfeeding. However, massage women tend to do two incorrect things:

1.   They sometimes press the mother's abdomen really hard, a practice that can lead to haemorrhage. So, tell them to do a very gentle circular motion on the

mother's belly, and just gently gather the loosened abdominal muscles with their palms towards the mother's navel.

2.   The hormones from the mother are still circulating in boy and girl babies, so their breasts are swollen with milk. Massage women tend to squeeze the breasts as a traditional practice. This can damage the soft tissue. As the hormone levels balance out, the swelling will subside. Instruct the massage woman not to do that.

Massage can be started a week after birth or when the stub of the umbilical cord falls off, and continued for forty days.

Q145. Is an enema compulsory before delivery?

Ans.   An enema is given as a routine practice in all hospital deliveries. In some instances, it may not be given if the mother delivers really quickly, before they have the time to give it.

Q146. Is it true that after two caesarean deliveries, the stomach tends to stay?

Ans. The stomach can stay after a normal delivery or after a caesarean delivery whether there be one or two deliveries. To prevent sagging of muscles, it is very important to exercise the muscles within the first forty days after delivery, when the stomach is very responsive to exercise because the body is still under the influence of relaxing hormones and is therefore more easily mouldable like plasticine. After a caesarean delivery, when the stitches are removed a week or ten days later, you can simply lie down with your legs bent at the knees, feet flat on the bed and take deep abdominal breaths. As you breathe in, inflate your stomach as much as you can, as you breathe out, deflate it as much as you can. That is, pull it in, as much as you can. Do at least five breaths at a time, a minimum of three times a day. You could do it before meals.

You can also, whenever you remember, stand tall and pull your stomach in and tighten your bottom and contract your pelvic floor, as when stopping urine from passing, at the same time. Done in the forty days or six weeks after the birth of the baby, it will give excellent results.

Q147. How many stitches do you normally get after a caesarean? Do they dissolve naturally or are they cut manually?

Ans. The number of stitches you get after a caesarean delivery will depend on the length of the scar. One scar is long and given from the navel down to the pubic hairline, and is called the vertical scar.

The second scar is smaller, like a dash above the pubic hairline. It is called the horizontal scar. The scars are stitched in layers. The stitches you eventually see are the ones right on the topmost layer of the skin. There are likely to be several underneath that dissolve. The topmost, external stitches are sometimes cut, and sometimes they dissolve. It depends on what kind of stitches your doctor gives you.

Q148. How many days does it take to recover from a normal delivery and a caesarean one?

Ans. After a normal delivery, the mother should recover from the discomfort of vaginal stitches in a week or ten days. After a caesarean delivery, a mother has her stitches removed a week or ten days after the birth. She further needs to be careful and not over-exert physically for at least six weeks. She has basically had an abdominal surgery, and post-operative care is required.

After both a normal and a caesarean delivery, the mother needs to stay at home and concentrate mainly on feeding the baby, for a minimum of four to six weeks.

Q149. How many days after delivery can one start taking pills as a method of contraception?

Ans. If along with breastfeeding you take the "progestogen only pill" or the minipill, it will help prevent conception, since it will be combined with reduced fertility produced by breastfeeding. You should not have the regular oestrogen-progestogen combined pill, since it will reduce milk production.

Q150. If one opts for a Copper T, when should one have it installed after delivery?

Ans. It can be inserted six weeks after the birth of the baby in a normal delivery.

Q151. How many days after delivery can one resume normal intercourse?

Ans. Your doctor will discuss contraception with you about six weeks after the birth of the baby. If you get copper T fitted forty days after the birth, you have a two year break from having to worry about contraception.

If intercourse happens before forty days, you could use another method, like a condom and a spermicidal gel. However, if you are breastfeeding your child hundred percent, the hormone levels in your body may prevent a pregnancy from happening.

Q152. Is it painful?

Ans.   Intercourse can be painful if your muscles are very tense and tight. In that case, you can try and relax your muscles by letting out a deep breath slowly and relaxing your jaw by separating your teeth. It is important that intercourse be preceded by a lot of loving, stroking and foreplay for it to be less painful. The foreplay lubricates the vagina with natural secretions so that intercourse is not painful. It is a very important part of pleasurable sex for both the partners.

Q153. What medically is the ideal age gap between two children?

Ans.   Medically, the ideal age gap between two children is three years, since it gives the mother time to recover her health and strength, and the first baby to get breast milk exclusively for up to two years, even though by two years, the baby might be having just one or two odd feeds. In a mother coming from an affluent background where she can eat good food, and a mother who is getting on in years so that she needs to have her babies quickly, or a mother who wants to quickly complete her family and get on with her career, the gap can be smaller.

Q154. Does one come to know of a stillborn child in advance?

Ans. Sometimes one can know it in advance and sometimes not.

Q155. Is it advisable to conceive soon after a miscarriage?

Ans. It is good if you can first have time to grieve for your lost baby before you can conceive again.

Q156. When does the normal cycle of periods begin after delivery?

Ans. After the birth of the baby, you will have a longish period lasting for a week or several weeks. Then, if you are breastfeeding, you may not have a period for several months. If you breastfeed exclusively on demand for the first few months, that is, if you give no other feed than breast milk, your period can take six to eight months to return. If you add complementary bottles and other food to your baby's diet, your period could return in two or four months. With unrestricted breastfeeding, your period could take a year to come.

Q157. If I do not have a period, does it mean I cannot become pregnant?

Ans. Even when you do not have a period, you can ovulate and become pregnant. On the other hand, some women may have a period or two that may not be accompanied by the release of an ovum or egg, that is, the periods will be anovular that cannot cause pregnancy.

Breastfeeding and menstruation are, therefore, unreliable indexes to whether you can conceive or not.

5
You and the Baby: Breastfeeding

Q158. Should the baby not go to the nursery after it is born?

Ans. Only a baby needing special care needs to go to the nursery. That would mean a premature baby, a baby weighing less than 2.25 or 2.50 kilograms, etc.

In fact, latest research shows that special care babies thrive best under "kangaroo care", that is, when they are placed between the mother's breasts, and the mother is given a loose gown to wear.

Q159. Does not keeping the baby in the room with the mother expose it to infections that the visitors may carry?

Ans. You cannot always keep the baby in a sterile environment. The baby has to learn to survive in the environment in which it is born. There is no point in over-protecting the baby, or else it will catch every infection when in school, when teething (as babies could chew on car keys, dirty toys, etc.), when exposed to any other child carrying an infection, and so on. The more the baby is exposed to infections, the more the baby can learn to fight it.

Moreover, the baby is fed the colostrum, a clear fluid present in the breast from the sixth month of pregnancy onwards, and for one or two days after the birth of the baby.

Although there is no milk in the mother's breast for the first few days, it is recommended that the mother suckles the baby at the breast anyway so that the baby gets the colostrum which passes to it all the immunities the mother carries. As a result, the baby withstands all the infections the mother can withstand, and hence it gets the immunity to fight infections that the visitors may carry, or infections that exist in hospitals. When colostrum turns into milk in a few days, the mother's milk continues to give the baby immunities to fight infections.

Q160. Why is it recommended to keep the baby with the mother in the room? Does she not need rest?

Ans.   Keeping the baby in the room with you is called "rooming-in" of the baby. Yes, the mother needs rest after the birth of the baby and the baby also needs rest after the experience of being born!

Maybe that is why Nature has planned it that the colostrum is very high in fat and protein. Even though it is very little in quantity, it gives the baby a very full feeling, and it is six to eight hours before the baby demands the next feed.

It takes a tremendous amount of effort for the baby to feed and adjust to experiencing the air around it, instead of the warm water in the womb. Therefore, babies lose weight in the first seven to ten days of their life. As the mother rests, so does the baby.

An added advantage of keeping the baby in the room with the mother is that, since a baby is born sterile, the bacterial flora of the mother will colonise the baby's body. If the baby is in the nursery, the bacterial flora of the nursery will colonise the baby's body, which is when you hear of babies catching nursery infections.

Q161. How long should one breastfeed?

Ans. For six months, exclusive breastfeeding is recommended. Thereafter, the baby starts other food and the breastfeeds are gradually reduced.

Breastfeeding can go on up to two years, with the baby having one to two feeds in twenty-four hours. Two years is recommended because the immunity from breast milk prevents serious illness in the baby while teething.

Q162. What if the mother is not able to breastfeed?

Ans. To be able to breastfeed successfully:

1. The mother should be willing to breastfeed.
2. The mother should be confident about breastfeeding.
3. The mother should be relaxed when breastfeeding.
4. The mother should have had previous preparation on how to breastfeed, or, she should have on the spot positive support to breastfeed.

Q163. What if the above points are not present?

Ans. It is possible that some mothers are not prepared for breastfeeding and are not very keen or confident about it. Such a mother can successfully breastfeed if she makes it a point to give the first breastfeed within one hour of birth and does not give the bottle to the baby at all, that is, if she exclusively breastfeeds and remains relaxed when feeding.

It will also help if the mother is well-nourished and drinks lots of fluids—milk, water, soup, anything. She does not need to drink lots of milk to make milk. Lots of sweetened and flavoured milk can make her put on weight. Plain milk is better.

Q164. What about diet when breastfeeding?

Ans. When a mother is breastfeeding, her diet should be nourishing. Spicy food is avoidable. She should also avoid cigarettes, strong or excessive intake of tea, coffee or alcohol.

Some mild tea, or a glass of mild beer or wine once a day is permissible. Soups can be had as can traditional beverages, like those made from boiling herbs or spices in water.

Traditional recipes that have herbs, nuts, dry fruits, seeds, edible gum, etc. are also good to eat. Most people shy away from such recipes because of their fat content. However, the fat content can be considerably reduced by roasting some of the ingredients instead of frying them. By roasting the *suji* or *atta* before adding *ghee* to it, the amount of *ghee* required can be reduced to half or less than half. If you cannot get traditional recipes made, continue to eat soaked almonds in the morning. Also eat other dryfruits, sprouts, seasonal vegetables, *dal* with *roti* or rice, porridge (dalia), *khichdi*, etc.

A breastfeeding mother needs more calories than a pregnant woman. This makes her very hungry. If she does not eat traditional preparations, she will crave for and eat stuff like ice-creams, pastries, *jalebies, gulab jamuns*, etc. which will be fattening, minus the nourishment of traditional fare.

Q165. If I consume hard food, i.e, *channa*, etc., will it make the baby's stomach upset?

Ans. Sometimes if you eat gaseous foods like *channa*, *rajma* or kidney beans, *gobi* or cabbage/cauliflower, the baby may get uncomfortable with wind or may have an upset stomach. Sometimes too much milk or alcohol taken by the mother can also upset the baby.

Q166. What if the mother's milk is not enough?

Ans. Mother's milk takes two to three days to come in the breast. Before that, colostrum is present in the breast—it is a clear fluid, very rich in immunities, fat and protein. On drinking colostrum, the baby may not ask for a feed for six to eight hours since colostrum is very rich and heavy. The mother needs to feed only when the baby demands it. In the first couple of days there are hardly any soiled nappies.

When the milk supply is established and the baby has a minimum of six wet nappies in twenty-four hours, it is a sign that the baby's milk intake is enough.

If a mother feels her milk is less, the best way to increase the milk supply is to feed more often, because each time she breastfeeds, she re-stimulates the production of more milk.

Q167. Does breastfeeding hurt?

Ans.   While feeding at the breast, the baby's gums press on the areola, that is, the dark area behind the nipple. The nipples get extended back towards the baby's gullet, and the baby's tongue 'milks' it by pressing it against the roof of the baby's mouth or palate.

If the baby 'munches' on the nipple instead of the areola, it will hurt the mother. If it does, the mother should break the baby's suck by inserting a finger into the corner of the baby's mouth or by pulling the chin down, in order to make the baby release the breast before she takes the baby off the breast. Then, when she offers the breast again, she should make sure the baby gets a bigger mouthful of it so that the baby latches on correctly, and its gums press on the areola, not on the nipple. When latching on is correct, there is no pain.

Q168. At what fixed gap should one feed the baby?

Ans. One should feed a baby on demand, that is, feed the baby when it cries to be fed or seems hungry. Forget the clock. The gaps between feeds can be erratic. The time the baby takes over a feed can vary from thirty to sixty to even ninety minutes!

Q169. What about babies who constantly demand breastfeeding?

Ans. Often there are babies who fake constant hunger. When put to the breast, they are playful or disinterested feeders. Such babies are actually demanding comfort sucking, not nutritive feeding. They probably have mothers who do not cuddle them between feeds and hold them only for the purpose of feeding. If the mother cuddles them between feeds, they will stop pretending to be hungry just to feel warm and secure. Sometimes if the mother is stressed, tense or depressed, the baby senses her anguish and wants to be constantly near her for reassurance.

Such babies cry a lot and seem to be hungry. Further, babies may actually be constantly hungry when they have a growth spurt, that is, when they grow taller or fatter. Their growth requires more milk, so they go through a temporary phase, of about two days approximately, when they want frequent feeding. This steps up the milk supply in the breast. Once the milk supply is increased, they go back to bigger gaps between feeds. At such times it is best for the mother to take two days off and go to bed with the baby and concentrate only on feeding for those two days.

Q170. Should one feed through the night?

Ans.   Until the baby weighs ten pounds, it requires feeding on demand which could mean two to three hour intervals. When it gains ten pounds, it can go without a feed for five to six hours. At that time you can try to increase the gap between night feeds.

Q171. If I express breastmilk and keep to feed the baby, will it not spoil without boiling?

Ans.   You never boil breast milk; boiling makes it lose its properties.

Expressed milk will stay unspoilt at room temperature for six to eight hours even in summer.

It will stay in the fridge for twenty-four hours. When in the fridge, it separates into fat and water layers, but this does not mean it has got spoilt. Just stir it, warm it if you like and feed to the baby. If the milk is not really chilled, there is no harm in feeding the baby cold milk.

You can also freeze breast milk for one to three months. You could freeze it in ice cube trays and melt the cubes for use when required. Do not microwave the breast milk cubes or expressed breast milk, since the microwave heats unevenly and there may be pools of very hot milk that could burn the baby's tongue/mouth. If you have regular power supply, breast milk cubes will stay for three months. If the electricity goes off now and then, they stay okay for one month.

Q172. When does one start giving the baby top feed?

Ans. 'Top feed' does not necessarily mean bottle feed. Regular milk and milk products like custard, porridge, baked vegetables, *kheer*, etc. can be given to the baby after six months of exclusive breastfeeding.

Q173. Should the baby be given water in the first six months?

Ans. No, the baby doesn't need water in the first six months. It gets the required water through breast milk. The mother needs to drink plenty of water. The baby's stomach has a very small capacity. It is better to fill it with nutritive milk that also has water, rather than with water that has no nutrition and could bring with it contamination or infection.

Q174. I had stopped smoking during pregnancy. Can I continue to do so after delivery?

Ans.   It is important not to smoke or drink alcohol while breastfeeding. However, a glass of wine or beer once a day is permissible.

Q175. How long can I breastfeed?

Ans.   For six months, exclusive breastfeeding is recommended. Thereafter, the baby starts other food and the breastfeeds are gradually reduced.

Breastfeeding can go on up to two years, with the baby having one to two feeds in twenty-four hours. This is the best since it gives the baby less chances of falling ill when teething.

However, some women like to breastfeed only up to eight to twelve months.

Q176. Why does one get sore nipples?

Ans.   When you want to stop feeding, if you pull and drag the baby off the breast, it might give you sore nipples. So instead, you must break the baby's suction by putting the tip of your finger in the corner of the baby's mouth and then take him off the breast, or pull the chin of the baby downwards before removing it from the breast.

Further, if you press your breast down with the finger by forming a big dent on the breast, in order to prevent the baby's nose from getting blocked, the act of pressing the breast down will cause the nipple to project upwards and hit the roof of the baby's mouth when it feeds. This hitting of the nipple on the hard palate will cause it to get sore. Instead of denting the breast in this fashion, place your fingers under the breast and raise it slightly so that any bulge of the breast that is there goes backwards and meets with the chest.

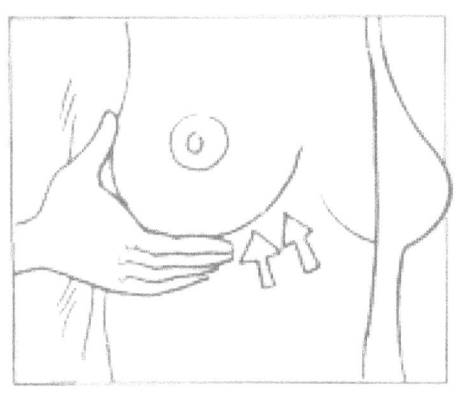

Soreness may also happen if the baby munches on the nipple instead of the areola, the dark area behind. Make sure the baby is latched on properly; by placing both the nipple and the areola well into the baby's mouth.

Soreness sometimes occurs if the nipples are frequently washed with soap. Water is sufficient to wash them.

Pressure applied at the same point constantly can also lead to soreness. It therefore helps to change positions during a feed, and to adopt different positions for different feeds so that pressure is applied to different points on the breast.

Soreness may be caused by a baby sucking too long after the breast has been emptied. The baby takes approximately twenty minutes of sucking time to empty a breast; after that he only indulges in comfort sucking. Restrict comfort sucking.

Q177. How do you help heal sore nipples?

Ans.   Soggy nipples, that is, nipples that remain wet for long periods, are more prone to soreness. It therefore helps to expose your nipples to air and sunlight as much as possible until the soreness heals. You can wear a loose garment without a bra.

Avoid using creams on cracked nipples. Dry cornflour can be dusted on them instead. It is also very helpful to express some milk after a feed and rub it on the sore nipple where it should be left to dry. This quickens healing considerably. Avoid the use of water-proof-backed bra pads. Do not remove any crust appearing on the nipple. It is part of the healing process.

Always offer the less sore side first. That will establish the flow on the sore side, before the baby takes it, thus making it less painful. You can use breathing for labour to be able to handle the pain.

An aspirin or a mild alcoholic drink like wine or beer taken shortly before a feed will help reduce the pain. It can be taken if the pain begins to interfere with the let down or release of milk.

You can try using a cold compress on your nipples before feeding. Apply an ice-cube wrapped in a towel or hanky. You can wear a blotting paper on an ever-dry nappy liner inside the bra to keep the nipples dry.

Sometimes a sore nipple may bleed. There is no harm if the baby swallows tiny amounts of blood with the milk. This can be quite frightening, especially when the baby burps after a feed and, along with the curdled milk, brings up a little blood. However, this is harmless to the baby. Continue to treat your sore nipples and carry on feeding.

There may be a risk of infection on sore nipples if the baby has thrush, that is, white spots on the tongue that do not wipe away. Thrush must be treated medically. You can take the baby off the breast for a few feeds until the skin has healed. The milk can be expressed and fed to the baby from a cup.

A nipple shield can be used. It is a rubber shield that fits over the nipple and areola and prevents direct suction on the nipple.

Q178. What happens if the nipples are flat or inverted?

Ans. Earlier this was considered to be a problem. However, this is not considered to be a problem anymore because, as the baby's gums come down on the areola, the dark area behind the nipple where the normal colour of the skin and the dark colour meet, the rest of the areola forms into the shape of a nipple as it gets milked between the baby's tongue and palate (roof of the baby's mouth). Milk squirts out of the tip of the nipple down the baby's throat.

Q179. Can I have medicines/drugs when I am breastfeeding?

Ans. Any medicine taken when breastfeeding should be taken under the doctor's supervision. Drugs taken by the mother may cause adverse reactions in the baby through the ingested breast milk.

Purgatives like senna, phenolpthalein may cause diarrhoea. Anti-epileptic drugs (barbiturates), opium or diazepam may make the baby drowsy. Smoking reduces the milk output. Hormonal contraceptives reduce the milk output; antihistamines cause drowsiness; metronidazole causes irritability weakness, blood dyscrasias and anorexia. The physician must therefore consider the benefits to the mother and possible dangers the baby may face each time a drug is prescribed during the nursing period.

Q180. How safe are breast implants for breastfeeding?

Ans. Silicon breast implants do not interfere with breastfeeding.

Q181. Is using the breast pump advisable?

Ans. Breast pumps are useful and effective when the breasts are overfull. There is an electric breast pump in hospitals which is effective.

There is a battery operated imported breast pump which is more effective when the breast is full of milk.

There is an Indian breast pump which looks like the horn of an auto rickshaw, that is, it has a rubber bulb and a funnel like glass at the other end. The funnel end is placed on the breast after the rubber bulb is pressed. The rubber bulb is then gently released and suction causes the release of milk. This should only be used when milk is to be discarded.

The rubber bulb cannot be sterilised and if the milk gets into it, it gets a strange bitter taste. You can express milk by hand, gradually over the whole day, and keep collecting what you express in the refrigerator. After twenty-four hours, change the glass and restart collection. This milk can be fed to the baby whenever you are busy.

Q182. Do newborn babies always have jaundice?

Ans. No, jaundice doesn't always occur in newborn babies. If it does occur, it should be treated.

Q183. Why do some new born babies have jaundice?

Ans. It can be a physiological reaction to the normalisation of the baby's haemoglobin levels. Physiological jaundice is fairly common, mild and usually harmless.

In the uterus, the baby has an extremely high level of red blood cells. Once the baby is born and starts breathing, the extra red blood cells are not needed. They break down until an appropriate level is reached. A by-product of the breakdown is bilirubin which can deposit in the baby's skin and/or eyes; and is seen as a yellow colouring. It normally appears thirty hours after birth, peaks around the fourth or fifth day, and disappears by the seventh day. In this jaundice, the bilirubin levels do not exceed 10 mg/100ml.

Jaundice can also be caused by the medication of a mother in labour. The baby gets the same medication through the placenta. The medication the mother receives is in accordance with her height and weight, and is therefore a massive overdose for the baby, who is a fraction of the mother's weight and height. This can cause a strain on the baby's liver.

Induction of labour can also contribute to jaundice in the baby, since it causes unnaturally strong contractions to occur. These exceptionally strong contractions shunt extra amounts of blood to the baby, resulting in jaundice.

Physiological jaundice is most common. Abnormal jaundice and breast milk jaundice are rare. They can occur within twenty-four hours of birth or at the end of the first week of life, respectively.

Q184. Is it true that reading after delivery can make the eyesight weak?

Ans. Light reading will not harm the eyesight but overstrain of any kind, be it long hours of reading, working on the computer, watching long hours of television, embroidery, etc. is avoidable.

Q185. What is the ideal weight of an infant in India?

Ans. A healthy infant born at term (thirty-eight to forty-two weeks) should have an average weight of 2.7 to 3.1 kilograms in India. A birth weight of less than 2500 gms is considered low.

Q186. Should one breastfeed the child when ill?

Ans. Cold, flu, fevers should not require you to stop feeding. Your body will make antibodies to fight the infection you have. Your baby will get these antibodies through breast milk and will therefore be protected from the infection. However, do let the doctor know that you are nursing the baby when he prescribes you medicines.

When feeding, antibiotics such as tetracycline and streptomycin, steroids, and sulpha-containing drugs should be avoided.

Some laxatives may cause colic and diarrhoea in the baby. Antithyroid drugs may cause goitre. Anti-coagulants and large doses of aspirin can cause bleeding problems in the baby.

Sedatives or tranquillisers, such as valium, can cause drowsiness and feeding problems.

Q187. Does breastfeeding decrease sexual desire?

Ans. No, breastfeeding does not decrease sexual desire.

Q188. Does feeding lead to sagging breasts?

Ans. If you wear a good supportive bra while feeding, breastfeeding need not cause the breasts to sag. Breasts can also sag with age or obesity, without ever nursing a child. Exercises for the breast can help them regain their shape if they do sag. These exercises should be done after you stop breastfeeding.

Q189. Is it true that one should wear a bra, twenty-four hours to prevent sagging?

Ans. No, at night one should remove the bra, but make sure you wear it through the day when you are walking about and exerting.

Q190. My baby doesn't burp.

Ans.   Burping depends on the amount of air a baby swallows. Breastfed babies do not swallow as much air as bottle-fed babies. Breastfed babies therefore burp less.

Q191. Can breastfeeding help me lose weight?

Ans.   Yes, breastfeeding can help you lose weight. The end milk in the breast is the fat rich milk or the milk with the *malai* or cream. The baby should have the end milk, apart from the watery milk that gushes in the beginning. The later part of the milk is that which is thicker and whiter and does not gush out, but if you press on the areola (the dark area behind the nipple), very white drops of milk appear on the nipple. In order that the baby gets the later milk, the mother should feed only from one breast and at the other breast only at the other feed.

This way the baby gets the end part of the milk which is fattening and makes the mother lose weight and the baby gain weight.

(*Note:* If the baby does not seem satisfied, the mother can feed briefly from the other breast also. Then at the next feed the mother can feed mainly at the breast she fed a little bit from.)

Q192. Why is it stressed that babies should be breastfed within thirty minutes of being born?

Ans.   Soon after birth, babies have a strong rooting and sucking reflex. If you just place the baby near the mother's breast, it will correctly attach to the breast for feeding (rooting reflex) and immediately start sucking at the breast (sucking reflex). This gives a good start to breastfeeding. The baby has successfully learnt the technique of sucking at the breast, and will do so effortlessly henceforth. The more the start of breastfeeding is delayed, the possibility of problems connected with breastfeeding is higher. For instance, if the baby is given bottle milk at the start, it can suffer from "nipple confusion" because when sucking at the breast, the baby has to "munch", but when sucking at the bottle, the milk drips regardless of the baby making an effort with its jaw.

Further, the five senses of the baby are very alert when the baby is born. This means, at birth the baby can smell well, hear well, see well, taste well and is very sensitive to touch. If these five senses are stimulated at birth, it causes certain stage specific (time-bound) connections to happen in the brain of the baby. These connections can happen at birth, or else they will never happen. When they happen, they give the baby better brain–body co-ordination for the rest of its life. They happen very spontaneously when the baby is held by the mother immediately after birth, since mothers automatically talk with the baby and look into the baby's eyes. When the baby is held closely by the mother, the baby smells the mother and if placed near the mother's breast, will automatically latch on to the mother's breast and start sucking the colostrum, thus stimulating the sense of taste. Hence, all the five senses get stimulated, and certain connections get made in the reticular formation of the baby's brain.

According to the book *Maternity Home Practices & Breastfeeding* by ACASH (Association for Consumers Action on Safety and Health), 'Babies who remain with their mothers for at least forty-five minutes within one to two hours of life, feed and gain weight more satisfactorily, speak at an earlier age and have a larger vocabulary at age two than babies who are separated from mothers after delivery'.

According to Dr Greenberg, Rosenberg and Lind of USA (1973), 'A study of impact of rooming-in on the mother revealed that the women who had the rooming-in experience were more self-confident with their infants, more competent in their care and could understand one or more attitudes of their baby's cry at the time of discharge when compared to no rooming-in mothers'.

Q193. Traditionally, breastfeeding is never started immediately after birth.

Ans. UNICEF's chief of health in India, Marzio Babille, blames superstition and cultural beliefs for denying babies the big immune boost that comes from colostrum (first breast milk). 'There is a belief that colostrum is bad for a baby, so in some states, a baby is fed water or honey diluted with water. Not only is this a missed opportunity but it's dangerous as the water or the spoon could be contaminated.'

In India, child malnutrition is mostly the result of a high level of exposure to infection and inappropriate feeding and caring practices, and has its origin almost entirely during the first two to three years of one's life.

A recent study of more than ten thousand new-born babies, published in the American journal "Pediatrics", has shown that if all babies start breastfeeding within one hour of being born, neonatal deaths will be reduced by twenty-two percent.

Breastfeeding can save the lives of 2.5 lakh newborn babies a year, in India.

Q194. I don't understand why people are so hung up on breastfeeding these days.

Ans.   For twenty-five years USA opposed breastfeeding, but now they find obesity costs are too high. Yes, bottle feeding can lay the seeds of obesity. Since the bottle drips milk regardless of the baby's appetite, the baby gets used to over-eating. The fat cells that get formed at that age are very stubborn and difficult to get rid of in later years.

In breastfeeding, the baby makes an effort to drink milk by exercising its jaws only till it is hungry. Breastfed babies are therefore less likely to be overfed. Also, breastfed babies are known to have higher IQ (Intelligence Quotient), mathematical ability and analytical ability.

Q195. I don't like the idea of the baby being at the breast always.

Ans. You do not have to have the baby at the breast always. You can express breast milk and it can be fed to the baby when you are sleeping or out of the house.

Expressed breast milk could be fed either from a glass or with a cup and spoon to the baby.

When using a glass, make sure it is a small glass with a round, smooth edge. It should not have a sharp edge.

A small *katori* (bowl) with a smooth edge can also be used. Put some expressed milk in the glass, cup or bowl. Place the baby with the head slightly raised on your lap. Place the edge of the bowl at the baby's lower lip and tilt till the level of milk reaches the lips of the baby. The baby will sense its presence and lap it up by sticking its tongue out, just like a puppy or a dog slurps up milk or water by sticking its tongue out! When the level of the milk goes down, tilt some more. Initially, if given to a baby who has already had a bottle, the baby is likely to protest by flaying its arms. This might drop some milk, so make the baby wear a bib before trying it for the first time, or ask someone to hold the baby's arms. The alternative would be to swaddle the baby or wrap it in a sheet so that its arms do not flay. Gradually, the baby will become adept at it.

You could also feed the baby with a small spoon after positioning it on your lap as described above. A *paladi* or traditional feeding cup can also be used.

As the baby grows, apart from expressed breast milk, soups, juices, water, milk or any other liquid can be fed in a similar way.

Feeding from a glass is best because the baby's tongue moves exactly as when breastfeeding. Besides, the baby needs to make an effort for every sip it takes, so it does not get used to over-feeding.

Q196. How does one express breast milk?

Ans. One can express breastmilk manually, that is, with one's hands. When breastfeeding, the flow of milk is already established, so that is a good time to express milk by pressing where the dark skin and the normal coloured skin meet. Never press on the nipple. If the breasts are leaking milk, that is another good time to express milk.

One can also use a battery-operated or a manual breast pump, in which case all parts used will have to be properly sterilised by boiling. Do not use sterilising solutions; babies get used to their smell and will not take milk if the smell is absent. Besides, we must not have the baby ingest a daily dose of sterilising solution.

Hospitals and nursing homes have electric breast pumps which can be used to express colostrum or breastmilk to be sent to a baby under special care in an intensive care nursery.

Q197. What difference does it make if the baby is not kept with the mother when born?

Ans. According to the book *Maternity Home Practices & Breastfeeding* by ACASH (Association for Consumers Action on Safety and Health), 'When infants were three months old, detailed observations at home have revealed that early contact mothers spent significantly more time looking after their infants, face to face, kissing them, whereas control mothers spent more time cleaning their babies'.

Q198. Why is there so much of stress on breastfeeding today?

Ans. New born care is synonymous with breastfeeding. Therefore, breastfeeding has a high priority for care of the sick new born.

In India, the Tenth Five Year Plan has breastfeeding as a national goal, and there has been a thirteen percent improvement in the survival of children under five years of age, with exclusive breastfeeding.

Exclusive breastfeeding for the first six months results in the baby receiving appropriate nutrients in adequate quantity and promotes the most favourable growth of children.

Q199. Is it not too much to expect from the mothers?

Ans. Mothers can manage breastfeeding quite comfortably if they have family support. They need extra help to take care of the routine household chores for at least six weeks. They can also express milk which can be fed by someone else, if they need to sleep or go out.

After six months, babies should start getting other food too, preferably home cooked food, for instance, *dal, khichdi, kheer, halwa, upma* or fruits like mashed banana (babies like slightly overripe bananas), mango, chikoo, etc. according to the season.

You can start a new food once a week, say every Monday or Tuesday. If the baby has an allergic reaction to any food, you will be able to get medical help easily on weekdays. Every once a week, you will add either *dal*, rice or wheat, and those things can then be fed to the baby by care givers when you are away or busy.

Packed foods should not be given to babies as they are exceptionally smooth in texture, and once babies get used to it, they reject home food. Home food has a tremendous variety and therefore caters more to the nutritional needs of the baby.

Malnourishment is less likely in babies fed from the family pot. Besides, home food is fresher and minus preservatives. You can roast rice or wheat on a *tawa* and dry grind it. Use that powder with either *dal*/milk/water and cook like a porridge to feed the baby.

When travelling or visiting friends/relatives, ask them to keep some *dal* without *tarka* for you. Put the *dal* with a chappati in a mixie and make a mash of it, or soak pieces of chappati in the dal till they become soft and then mash with a fork. Add some *ghee* or butter to it and feed the baby.

Q200. How can a mother breastfeed when travelling?

Ans. When travelling, the mother finds it convenient to breastfeed because she does not need to find a kitchen, clean water and pots, nor does she have to spend time in preparing a feed. It gives her freedom to move without being dependent. It also reduces the chances of the baby falling ill.

Q201. What are the advantages of breastfeeding?

Ans. Breastfeeding has a number of advantages for the mother. Breastfeeding at birth reduces blood loss after delivery by making the uterus contract. Exclusive breastfeeding delays conception of the next child and therefore contributes to natural birth spacing. It also reduces the risk of cancer of the reproductive tract in the mother in later life, that is, cancer of the uterus/ ovaries/etc.

Q202. What if the breastfeeding mother has AIDS (acquired immune deficiency syndrome)?

Ans. In AIDS, the baby should be given either exclusive breastfeeding or exclusive top feeding.

In poor, poverty-stricken areas, the mother should exclusively breastfeed because the risk of death in the infant's first year is fifty percent from diarrhoea and other diseases, not including AIDS. On the other hand, the risk of dying from AIDS when born to AIDS infected mother is only eighteen percent. In clean affluent homes where sterilisation procedures, clean water, etc. are possible, the mother can give animal milk to the baby.

Q203. What if the mother is HIV positive?

Ans.   A study was done in Zimbabwe, Africa. In Zimbabwe, thirty percent of the population is HIV infected. Exclusive breastfeeding in the first six months was found to reduce HIV transmission. Breastfeeding beyond six months is not recommended for HIV positive mothers.

The introduction, before the age of three months, of solid foods or animal milk to breastfeeding infants, born to HIV positive mothers, was found to increase the risk of transmission of HIV infection to the baby.

After the age of six months, the maximum transmission of HIV infection starts. Therefore, the study showed that the more strictly HIV positive mothers breastfeed, especially for six months, the lower the risks of HIV or death for their infants.

Q204. What are the dos and don'ts, in case the mother is HIV positive?

Ans.   The baby should be breastfed exclusively for the first six months and after six months, breastfeeding should be stopped.

Safe sex, that is the use of condoms while the mother is breastfeeding, is recommended in order to avoid re-infection of the mother.

The mother should be well-prepared, counselled or trained to breastfeed successfully in order to avoid cracked nipples or mastitis.

If the mother can afford strict cleanliness and sterilisation, she can give animal milk.

Only sixty-three percent of babies born to HIV positive mothers could get infected. Seven percent can get infected during pregnancy. Fifteen percent can get infected during delivery. After six months of the delivery, maximum transmission to the baby starts.

Q205. What are the HIV statistics in India?

Ans.   In India, as of now, 2005-2006, there is only one percent to five percent presence of HIV in the different states.

Andhra Pradesh, Tamil Nadu, Maharashtra, Karnataka, Gujarat and the north-east states of Imphal, Manipur, etc. have most cases of HIV.

Q206. How does one test oneself to find out if one has HIV?

Ans. The Elisa HIV test can be done to find this out. If it shows a mother is HIV positive, two more tests are done to confirm it.

It is important that those who test HIV positive, and are scheduled for further testing, are given counselling.

Q207. What about risk to the baby?

Ans. The drug nevirapine given to the mother in labour, and to the baby after birth, reduces the chances of transmission of HIV to the baby. Exclusive breastfeeding for the first six months also reduces the chance of transmission.

For babies, the Elisa HIV test can be done at three, six, twelve and eighteen months to check for transmission.

Q208. What are the different options of feeding a baby?

Ans. **Breastfeeding:** Exclusive breastfeeding is best for the baby's health and growth. From six to twelve months, it provides half the baby's nutritional needs. Between one to two years, it provides one third of the baby's nutrition. Breastfeeding alone provides the baby with all the necessary nutrients and water up to six months.

Expressed Breast Milk Feeding: The mother can express her milk to be fed to the baby. The expressed milk can be fed to her own baby or someone else's baby.

Induced Lactation: If a woman has delivered a baby once in her lifetime, she can start producing milk again if she regularly suckles a baby to her breast.

Surrogate Mother or Wet Nursing: A breastfeeding mother can feed another mother's baby. This can be done for convenience or if the baby's mother is HIV positive.

Relactation: This happens when a breastfeeding mother resumes breastfeeding after a gap. If a mother suffers a loss in an accident, or if she experiences extreme stress as in an earthquake or a flood, her milk may stop temporarily. If she puts the baby to her breast to suckle, her milk starts flowing again. Besides, there is growing evidence that breastfeeding produces hormones that reduce tension and calm the mother and the baby.

Replacement Feeding: This means that the baby can be given formula milk (tinned milk) or fresh milk that the family normally uses. Besides, it implies feeding the baby other milk than the mother's milk. It could even be soya milk.

6
Alternative Systems for Mothers and Babies

Bach Flower Remedies

Background: Dr Edward Bach studied medicine at the University College Hospital, London. He was a House Surgeon there. Later, he started general practice at Harley Street, London, where he worked as a bacteriologist and later, a pathologist. He worked on vaccines.

He was dissatisfied with orthodox medicine where doctors were expected to concentrate on the diseases and ignore the people who were suffering them. He shifted to homoeopathy and wrote the famous bowel nosodes, still known as the seven Bach nosodes.

In 1930, he closed his lucrative Harley Street practice and left London. He decided to devote the rest of his life to finding remedies that were from the lap of Nature and pure. He wanted the medicine to rely less on the product of diseases. This is how the Bach Flower Remedies were born. The following is an extract from the book, *The Medical Discoveries of Edward Bach, Physician*, by Nora Weeks, Keats Publishing Inc., Connecticut, 1979:

> From his own experiences and from watching others closely, Bach realized that man, ...was endowed with all the wisdom and knowledge necessary to guide him through his earthly life in the utmost happiness and joy and health, and that this wisdom was imparted to him through his intuition and instincts.

These were means of communication between man's higher self and his earthly personality and being of divine origin, were to be obeyed and trusted implicitly. Unhesitating obedience to these was the secret of health and happiness.

When the individual allowed the interference or suggestions of others to deter him from following his own inner convictions, then the conflicting states of mind—fear, indecision, hate and the like—assailed him, marring his happiness and affecting his health.

About the Bach Flower Remedies, the book further states:

He (Dr Edward Bach) first collected the vital energy of the plant from the dew, as Paracelsus had done centuries earlier. Then he collected it through spring water and sunshine. Thus he developed his healing system in a most complete and beautiful relationship with the healing powers around us in Nature.

About how Dr Bach made the medicines, it says:

None of the flowers contained the healing properties he sought, but he found that the dew from each plant held a definite power of some kind... To collect sufficient dew from individual flowers would be too laborious and take too long a time, so he decided to pick a few blossoms from a chosen plant and place them in a glass bowl filled with water from a clear stream, and leave it standing in the field in full sunlight for several hours (four hours).

This he did, and to his great satisfaction found the water was impregnated with the power of the plant, and was very potent.

The finished tincture made from flowers was then preserved in bottles that had half tincture and half brandy.

Some of the Bach Flower Remedies that can be used by pregnant women and young mothers are as follows:

Crab Apple: Works very well for itching and rashes in pregnancy or otherwise. It needs to be applied locally in a cream or moisturiser.

In a 500 ml bottle of moisturiser, put almost 20–25 drops of Crab Apple. Shake well and use regularly twice or thrice a day, as required.

Alternatively, take a blob of cream/moisturiser/oil on your palm, put about three drops of Crab Apple in it, blend together and apply.

When a new mother feels the 'yuk factor', i.e. she feels messy handling soiled nappies, sour burps, milk leaking from breasts, figure out of shape, etc. Crab Apple can help.

It can also be had to mitigate the after-effects of strong allopathic medicines like antibiotics.

Impatience: For aches and pains in pregnancy.

Impatience and Holly: Can be taken together in case of high blood pressure.

Rock Rose: For fear of pain or surgery before delivery.

Rescue Remedy: During delivery, for fainting or panicking.

Also can be had generally as an SOS, whenever required. Could be taken by anybody when feeling low, having a headache, after a fall or accident, when going for an interview, during stressful times, etc. It could be added to any of the other remedies.

Olive: For mental or physical exhaustion in pregnancy, labour, after birth, or general mental and physical exhaustion experienced by non-pregnant women and men.

Mustard: For fluctuating moods after delivery or otherwise.

Holly: For inability to connect with the baby after delivery. Can also be given to the first born child when the second child is born. Can be had to handle the stress of living in very close proximity with other people.

Walnut: For the change in lifestyle that comes with pregnancy or during breastfeeding. Also for a change of job, home, city and any other major change in one's life.

Star of Bethlehem: After delivery, give to the mother. For a child born by ceasarean section, give at any age. This medicine is for shock.

White Chestnut: Helps sleeplessness and a mind that is over-active and never rests, that just goes on 'talking'.

Dosage and Availability: These medicines will be available at a shop selling homoeopathic medicines. Sometimes they may have the number 30 written in front of them. It is okay, you can use them.

They are in liquid form. You can add four drops of medicine in any liquid, water/*lassi*/*nimbupani*, etc., mix it up and drink. You do not need to avoid eating and drinking other food before or after taking the medicine.

You can mix more than one medicine at a time, going up to eight medicines. Eight drops of Rescue Remedy can always be added to whatever is your prescribed medicine.

You need to repeat the medicine four times a day. Can be repeated at shorter intervals, more often if required, e.g. in labour.

Have the medicine for fifteen days at a stretch.

In chronic conditions, the medicine can be had for a month or more.

Tissue Remedies

Tissue Remedies were innovated by Dr Schuessler who was born in 1821. Tissue Remedies work by compensating the deficiency of inorganic salts in a person's body through their medicinal counterparts. A deficiency or imbalance of these salts within our bodies can cause certain symptoms. For further knowledge, I would recommend the book *The Twelve Tissue Remedies of Schuessler* by Boerick MD and Dewey MD. The book would be available at a shop selling homoeopathic medicines. They would also sell the twelve Tissue Remedies.

Some of the useful Tissue Remedies are:

Ferrum Phos. 3x: Crush the tablets and put on a bleeding wound to instantly stop the bleeding. It works well for children and adults.

•   It can increase the haemoglobin levels in anaemic people.
•   In diseases that appear suddenly, it is to be taken in the early stages for all inflamed and feverish conditions.

Kali Phos 6x: Helps when there is sleeplessness, depression, nervousness, exhaustion from overuse of the brain.

There are certain mixtures of tissue salts that are patented and useful for certain conditions.

Bio Combination 26: It is to be had for an easy delivery and a safe and comfortable pregnancy.

A student of mine was recommended by a homeopath to have one dose of it once a day in the first week of the ninth month, two doses twice a day in the second week of the ninth month, three doses thrice a day in the third week, and four doses four times a day in the fourth week of the ninth month.

Bio Combination 25: It can be had instead of digene for acidity and flatulence.

Bio Combination 24 or Five Phoses: It can be given to irritable or ill children, and also to children who are teething. Adults can have it when feeling low or when they are getting a bodyache and feeling feverish. It can be had after delivery if the mother is suffering from nervous exhaustion.

Dosage and Availability: These medicines will be available at a shop selling homoeopathic medicines. One dose will be three tablets. Place the tablets under your tongue and allow them to melt. In an emergency, they can be taken more frequently, e.g. in fever, Ferrum Phos can be taken hourly. You could also dissolve a dose in water and go on sipping the water slowly. If confused, consult a practising homoeopath. These medicines do not expire. When they turn brown in colour, you can consider them expired.

Homoeopathy

Dr Samuel Hahnemann is the father of homoeopathy. Homoeopathy is based on the principle 'Similia simlibus curentur', or the premise that like cures like. In a way, it is similar to the principles of immunisation. Dr Hahnemann administered drugs to healthy individuals and noted the symptoms they displayed as a result of it. The same drug would cure similar symptoms in people who were ill, when administered in diluted homoeopathic doses.

Sepia 200: It is recommended for nausea at the sight and smell of food and for gas with bloated abdomen and sour burps. Have one dose daily for three days or seven days as required.

Arnica 30, Caulophyllum 30 and Cimicifuga 30: According to Dr Kamla Tiwari from Auroville, in the last month of pregnancy, these three medicines should be had weekly by a mother who is trying to have a normal delivery after a caesarean section. On day one of the first week of the ninth month, have Arnica 30, one dose; on day two, Caulophyllum 30, one dose; and on day three, Cimicifuga 30, one dose. Repeat likewise on day one of the second week, and subsequent weeks.

In the last week before the estimated date of delivery, take all the three medicines in the 200 potency. During labour, Pulsatilla 30 can be had hourly along with monitoring in a hospital.

These medicines will facilitate an easy delivery. Arnica will reduce the trauma, Caulophyllum will ensure proper working of the muscles of the uterus and Cimicifuga will reduce the pain.

Pulsatilla: Further, according to Dr Tiwari, if a mother has gone over her due date or estimated date of delivery, then the medicine Pulsatilla will help.

Give the mother one dose of Pulsatilla 200 on day one. Repeat another dose of Pulsatilla 200 on day two. On day three, give the mother one dose of Pulsatilla 1 M. It will cause labour to begin.

According to Dr Kamla D Patel, for an easy delivery, give Pulsatilla 30 to the mother in the seventh month;. Pulsatilla 200 in the eighth month and Pulsatilla 1 M in the ninth month. Each is to be had three doses for one day. In labour, give one dose of Pulsatilla 1 M every one hour for an easy delivery. Pulsatilla is also useful in positioning the baby correctly, if it is not in a head down position in late pregnancy.

Gelsemium 30: According to Dr Kamla D Patel from Anand, Gujarat, this medicine will help to reduce the fear felt by a first time mother in anticipation of labour. Have one dose a day. If not better, have one more dose the next day.

Caulophyllum 30: Dr S.K. Mankad from Mumbai recommends this medicine for easy delivery. In the beginning of the ninth month or the thirty-sixth week, take three doses three times a day. This medicine helps the opening up of the mouth of the uterus.

Arnica Ointment: Is very useful to use on babies if they fall off the bed and get a bump on their head. If you rub Arnica ointment, the bump on the head will disappear in a few hours.

It can also be used by pregnant mothers to apply on random pains on their back, thighs, under the ribs, etc.

Calendual Q: Q means the mother tincture form of the medicine. A few drops of calendula Q, maybe five or ten, maybe added to a mug of water to wash wounds where the skin has been cut. It heals dramatically, reduces scarring and the wound heals without getting septic. It can be used on stitches, cuts and bruises, and for washing fresh wounds before they are dressed.

Dosage and Availability: These medicines will not be available at a regular chemist shop. They will only be available at a shop selling homoeopathic medicines, and there are such shops all over India.

They are available Indian made and German made. They are available in liquid form and in the form of little sugar pills. For someone who is not allowed to take sugar due to a diet restriction, five drops of it straight into the mouth should be fine.

If one is taking the sugar pills, four pills at a time would make one dose. Ideally, place the dose under the tongue and let it melt. You are not to swallow them or bite them. You should rinse your mouth before taking the medicine, and avoid eating for about thirty minutes before or after taking the medicine.

The liquid medicine will be available in half and one ounce packing. The pills are sold in measures of drams. A one dram bottle is a small bottle roughly the length of a toothpick. A two dram bottle is twice its size.

If you are better, do not repeat the medicine because being healthy, you might display other symptoms of the drug.

If you experience an aggravation, stop taking the medicine. Since like cures like, the symptoms may aggravate but the aggravation will be short and sweet, after which the cure will be permanent. The aggravation should not extend beyond a couple of days. These medicines do not expire. If the pills start looking brownish in colour, then you can consider that the medicine has expired.

Caution: In homoeopathy, never go from a higher potency to a lower one. For example, if you take Pulsatilla 200 and follow it with Pulsatilla 30, the effect of the medicine will not be there. However, you can go from a lower potency to a higher one to enhance the effect of the medicine, that is, you can go from Pulsatilla 30 to Pulsatilla 200.

Index

www.ingramcontent.com/pod-product-compliance
Lightning Source LLC
Chambersburg PA
CBHW072207060526
44654CB00047B/1459